Wizard Quest

Hatchet and the Black Dragon

Book 6 in The GIFT Series

by

Suzanne de Board

Cover idea – Suzanne de Board

Cover Artist and Designer - Mary DeSantis

Author's photograph by Ryan Brewer

ISBN- 978-0-9989905-7-6

Library of Congress Control Number: 2019917957

Pen Pearls Books

Victorville, California

Also by Suzanne de Board

Pen Pearls – A Personal Anthology

The Gift – Book One in The Gift series

Merlin's Revenge – Book Two in The Gift series

The Revealing – Book Three in The Gift series

In the Beginning . . . Todd – Book Four in The Gift series

The Final Battle – Book Five in The Gift series

The Girl with the Sky-Blue Eyes

(prequel to The Gift series– Book one)

Return from Dragon Island

(Book two in the prequel to The Gift series)

Sarah Jane

Butterfly Girl

The House at Pine-Apple Woods

Lisa – Mystery at Waverly Manor

I Used to Be Me

The Spider's Veil – A Fairy Tale

The Table

Flora, Fauna, Frogs and More

(a coffee table book of Art and Photography)

Suzanne's Family Recipes

(a Cookbook)

Earth, Sky, and Sea

(a coffee table book of Art and Photography)

Chapter Books

Bumble Frog
Maya – Bay of the Dolphin
The Mice and the Wheat
The Drummer Boy and the Terrier
(Historical Fiction)
Treasure at Mermaid's Cove

Picture *Books*

Clarence Catches a Cold
Clarence Catches a Cold - a coloring book
Five Little Froggies
The Little Fish
The Little Fish – a Coloring Book
The Rainbow Bird
Priscilla's Worm

Books Coming Soon

The Christmas Party – Book 2
Lost and Found – Book 3
Ebony – The Kitten Who Saved the Day

Wizard Quest

Hatchet and the Black Dragon

by

Suzanne de Board

Hatchet

She watched him as he played, if one wished to call it that. Her eyes shone with love, mixed with concern, for her only son. She had named him William – a good name, a strong name, after his father . . . who some would say was not a good man. A thief . . . a bully . . . but still she had loved him. And now Willie seemed to be following in his father's footsteps. She prayed he would not meet his father's fate.

She found her love, one day, hung by his neck from a tall old oak. What had he done to deserve such a fate – steal a chicken or two? That was hardly worth death, and besides, he was only trying to provide for his family. He did as his father had done, and *his* father before him. On the eve before their wedding, he disappeared. He was going to change his life, be a proper husband and father, but the town folk couldn't see his goodness, his desire to be a decent, loving man. They killed him, hung him – and all for a couple of miserable chickens. So, she was left to raise their son alone. Will cried himself to sleep, that night, and swore revenge on those responsible. But he was just a boy. He didn't mean what he was saying.

He resembled his father to a point, but he was small for his age, and thus teased, unmercifully, at times. She was happy when he finally made a few friends, friends who would stick together and protect each other, no matter what, but still she worried.

These boys were trouble. She could feel it in her bones. They were wild, unruly, but they seemed to like Will, almost to worship him. Misfits, all of them, but determined to make something of themselves . . . whatever it took.

She gasped as Will grabbed a younger boy and held a small ax to his throat. *No*, she cried from within, and breathed a huge sigh of relief when the ax dropped to his side and he pushed the boy away.

"Hatchet . . . Hatchet . . . Hatchet," the boys began to chant, as the chastised child ran into the nearby woods, sobbing, and wiping at the small drops of blood dripping down his neck.

Hatchet . . . Hatchet . . . Hatchet . . . . The words reverberated through her mind. *Oh, my son. You are a good boy, not an evil one. Please . . . do not make me die of grief should you, as well, meet your father's fate.*

***

The boy, glancing back at his mother, held up the small ax, and grinned. Finally, he had respect, even if it stemmed from fear.

He would become a great leader and surely avenge his father's death, and his mother's poverty. With a mighty whoop, he chased after the terrified boy.

CHAPTER ONE

Five years later:

Hatchet stared at the wanted poster and frowned.

"Not a very good likeness, is it?"

Hatchet stiffened and slowly turned, his hand on the handle of his weapon of choice.

"Here, let me fix it for you." Alfred, the young wizard, pulled a wand from his tunic pocket, and carefully glancing about, pointed it at the poster. A curly mustache, and a short goatee now graced the face of the teen in the poster. A slightly balding hairline, and large ears, sticking out from the sides of his head, finished the composition. But now the young outlaw looked at least ten years older.

"Why'd ye do tha'?" the boy asked, mistrust, mixed with fear, clouding his eyes. Alfred had grown, tall and slender, and ever since he began to learn magic, he no longer seemed to fear the bully, the self-appointed leader of the gang.

"Come, come, Willie, it's just me. No need to fear an old friend."

"Don't call me Willie," The teen snarled. "'atchet's me

name, and don't y' be fergettin' it. W'at ye be doin' 'ere anyways?"

"I'm in need of your assistance . . . Willie."

Hatchet sighed. "Me assistance? W'at do ye be meanin', ye bein' a wizard an' all?"

"I am to be attached to the new king, as his personal wizard, and as we are old chums, as well as, well . . . you know, I need you to promise me you will cease your villainy and help bring peace to the kingdom. As you are aware, the young princess, Bee, will soon no longer be able to join us in our games, so things need to change."

"She is bein' *yer* frien', no' mine."

"Yes, and a lovely person she is, but she will soon be eighteen, and we will have to wait until the next generation is born before the adventures can begin anew. We may both be old before the new princess arrives."

"Perhaps a wee spell cud ke'p us both young."

"It doesn't work that way."

The outlaw let his hand drift to the handle of his ax, and smirked.

"Hatchet, my man. Do as you are told, and I may reconsider. And put away that weapon. You know, as well as I, you have no power over me. On the other hand . . ." he smiled shrewdly at the outlaw, "it would be best to harness your temper. It is, after all, because of your father and his, um, unfortunate death, I even give you the time of day."

"W'at do ye know about me fath'r. A gud man he was, and don't you be disrespectin' 'im;"

"Hatchet, your father was a bully and a thief. Your mother deserved better. You were too young to really know him, and I know your mother, my cousin by marriage, knew his true self, even though she loved him, and put up with his shenanigans. For what curious reason, I know not. Now, be a good boy and promise me you will behave yourself, lest you fulfill your own destiny and die like your father. If you determine to continue in your ways, perhaps I should change the poster back to its original state or correct it to show the real you. Look, here comes the constable. Well, what is it going to be?"

"I cud kill you right here, and be done wit' it," the outlaw growled.

"Tsk, tsk," Alfred answered, raising his wand toward the poster.

"A'right, a'right, oi'll do yer biddin' fer now, but there will be comin' a day . . . ."

"Yes, dear cousin, but until then, I expect you to behave, and I will protect you as best I am able."

"Me 'atchet will protect me."

"Have it your way, but don't be foolish, a little magic can always be useful . . . for good . . . or bad."

"Stolen magic." Hatchet groused.

"It matters not how it was acquired, just that I know how to use it, and you don't."

"Kin oi see the magic room . . . where you got it? Where all the fancy stuff comes from?"

"And what good would it do? You would just attempt to steal from the outside world, and that could cause a great deal of harm, for me as well as yourself . . . and our world. No, I think it best I keep certain things just between myself, the princess and Sirena. You would like her, Sirena that is. She is quite beautiful, but she is rather angry at the moment, so it would not be a good time for an introduction. Do we have a deal?"

Hatchet glanced toward the rapidly approaching constable and snarled. "Yes, Marster Alfred, we 'ave a deal . . . for now."

"Marster? What is marster? The word is Master Alfred."

"Thou art no master o' mine, and Marster is as gud as oi kin do."

"Then Marster it is. After all, what's in a name? As long as we know which side our bread is buttered on, what matters the name? Good man, *Willie*, or Hatchet, as it may be." He glanced toward the outlaw's weapon and smiled drolly. "I expect great things out of you, and if you play your cards right, who knows . . . ? I will call you when I need you. Good-bye for now."

Hatchet glanced toward the poster and smiled. He was unrecognizable, and the constable almost upon them. He turned to thank his cousin, but Alfred was gone. Only the imprints of where he once had stood, remained.

The constable didn't seem to have noticed the missing wizard as he approached the man at the tree. "Ho, there, man. You haven't seen the likes of anyone meeting this description, have you?" nodding toward the poster.

"No' I, your constableship. Sorry I canna be of 'elp."

The constable sighed. "Well, if ye do, it would be in your best interest to let me know. There's a reward on this fellow, dead or alive. Five hundred gold pieces."

"Five 'undred? Tha's a mighty fine bounty. Oi'll keep me eyes op'n."

The constable stared suspiciously at the young man. "See that you do."

Hatchet smiled as the constable walked off muttering to himself. "Yes, sir, oi'll keep me eyes wide op'n, yes oi will."

CHAPTER TWO

Hatchet shifted uncomfortably in the small chapel, as the priest droned on and on, uniting in marriage Alfred and his lady love, Magdalyn. He would never have chosen to be at this wedding, but as Alfred's only available relative, he had to be there, as a reluctant witness, if nothing else. This marriage was a secret, and Hatchet loathed secrets, unless they were his. Her family didn't approve, but Alfred was in love, and no one could stand in his way. When Alfred wanted something, Alfred always got what he wanted . . . or so it seemed.

He stared at the ring offered to Alfred from Magdalyn, as her marriage token. An odd-looking ring—beautiful, but odd. Its brilliant orange stone seemed to glimmer, and sparkle, far more than an ordinary stone, and the ring seemed far too big for Alfred's refined fingers. He blinked, and then blinked again as the ring seemed to shrink, until it fit exactly the young wizard's hand.

There be somethin' strange aboot tha' ring, he thought to himself, *or are me eyes playin' tricks on me?* With a sigh he dismissed the anomaly as an illusion of some sort, and once again began to pace in place.

"Stop it," Alfred hissed. "Hold still. You're making me nervous."

"I canno' help it," Hatchet whispered back. "Let's get this ov'r wit' so oi kin get meself outta here." He glanced nervously toward the chapel door and breathed a sigh of relief, as the priest finally droned – "You may now kiss your bride. You are one."

Hatchet turned and hurried toward the door.

"Where are you going?" Alfred asked.

"Th' deed is done, and oi am gone, if it pleases your lordship."

"Thank you, Will. But, before you go, you will need to sign the certificate . . . please . . . as the witness, you know."

Hatchet grabbed the pen and scribbled a quick X on the marriage certificate. "There, kin oi go now?"

"By all means. Here," smiled Alfred, still holding the hand of his beloved. "Let me help you. And thank you . . . cousin. I will not forget you."

Hatchet nodded, and as he exited the chapel, he disappeared and found himself on the outskirts of his own village, near his mother's hovel.

He hurried up the dirt pathway and entered his mother's

home. "Mama," he cried, rushing to her side as she lay still on the wood slat floor. "Mama, wat 'appened?" he probed as he gathered her into his arms.

"The . . . magistrate . . . came by, not . . . an hour ago," she whispered. "They have taken . . . our home . . . from us. We have no place . . . to go. I . . . have prepared . . . our last meal . . . then we . . . must . . . go, before the magistrate returns . . . and takes us to . . . the debtor's . . . prison. I am . . . so sorry, my son. I . . . I should . . . have done . . . better . . . by you."

Hatchet wept as his mother's eyes closed and she was no more. "Ye did yer best . . . Mama," he sobbed. "First they kilt Papa, and now they 'ave as gud as kilt you. They *all* will pay, Mama, jest see if they don't." He held her still body in his arms and cried, until there were no more tears.

***

Alfred ran from door to door, frantically searching for a doctor, a midwife, anyone who could come and help his beloved Magdalyn. It had been a year since she had become his wife, and her news of his impending fatherhood, was the happiest day of his life, next to their wedding. But now she was in trouble, with a difficult birth, and there was no one willing to help. *Surely there is one midwife in the village who will be willing to help, even if it is the middle of the night. That's what they're for, isn't it?*

Finally, he gave up and rushed back to her side. A tiny ball of wails lay by her side, and she was drenched in blood.

"P-promise me," she groaned weakly, "you will . . . care . . . for our precious . . . son . . . your son. And when . . . he is older, teach him . . . the properties . . . of the ring, for it is . . . his . . . inheritance." And she was gone.

"No, no, no," he cried, as he gathered her into his arms and sobbed. "Don't leave me. I cannot live without you." But there was not a sound, or movement, from his beloved.

The cries of the babe interrupted his grieving, and he stared at the wailing child. "It's all your fault," he screamed, flinging his arm to one side. "Get out of my sight . . . forever."

His eyes widened in horror, as the tiny bundle disappeared, and he was left alone. "No, no, no," he cried once again, horrified at what he had just done. "Come back! Come back! It wasn't you. It was them." But the child was gone, and he was left alone.

His heart froze that day, and he determined to make the village pay . . . not only for the loss of his beloved wife, but also for the loss of their precious son, for he knew not where their child had been sent. He was alone . . . so very alone.

***

And so, it began. Alfred changed his name to Merlin, for what reason Hatchet didn't know. But as long as he continued to look the other way, when a bit of pilfering was about, and stayed out of his business, Hatchet didn't care. It was those times Alfred didn't look the other way that irritated the outlaw.

He continued to call his cousin Marster, though it rankled him something fierce. But at least Alfred didn't expect to be called master. He, Hatchet, would never call him Master. No one was master of his life, and no one would ever be. He would bow to no one, especially a man who thought himself better than his only remaining relative. He would never submit to Alfred, unless it suited him . . . and for now it must suit him. Alfred was an ally he really couldn't do without – for the time being, anyway.

Marster. Even the thought of the 'endearment' left a bad taste (stench) in his mouth. But it was, after all, only symbolic. It didn't mean a thing, other than keeping Alfred happy . . . for a time. A master he would never have, he was master of his own life, but if it kept him out of prison, and allowed him to do what he did best, so be it.

Alfred thought *he* was in control, and Hatchet would, for the time being, allow him to think that way, but when the time came, and he knew deep in his heart it would, things would change for the better . . . Hatchet's better, that is. Then, yes, then, Alfred would be put in his place and he would be calling Hatchet, Master. The outlaw smiled. Someday . . . he could hardly wait.

***

Hatchet wiped his knife on his breeches, leaned back against a gnarled pine, and watched the men around the campfire. Good men, everyone, and each with his own expertise. They had gained quite a name for themselves, as of late. He knew it to be true, because the posters said so.

He was worth a lot more, today, than he had been when Alfred first made him promise to be honest and trustworthy. But that was before . . . before the loss of his cousin's wife and son. Now, he wasn't really much better than Hatchet, himself.

Alfred pretended to be a good and trustworthy wizard—for king and country—but had a tendency to look the other way when he, Hatchet, and his band of outlaws, did their dirty deeds. If the truth were told, it wasn't a bad idea, having a wizard for a cousin, especially one as powerful as Alfred. A wizard who would look the other way, when it proved most useful. Besides, Alfred loved the games . . . when the new princesses arrived.

The adventures always stepped up when a princess

from the outside world was present . . . to solve any mysteries or prevent the simplest of crimes. There were times, however, when said princess could be a real nuisance, and Alfred always seemed to take the side of the outsider, even before family. That could be a problem, but it was all pretend, wasn't it?

Many years had passed since the second princess had ceased her visits, and life was back to where it should be. However, the land seemed to be somewhat different as of late. The little creature, Todd, was rarely seen, and the dark wood was becoming a dreary place. He missed having an outsider princess to liven things up. Perhaps Alfred could hurry things up a bit.

He paused, cocking his head to one side. *Wha' was tha'? Th' sound o' a meadow lark?* Hatchet giggled like a little girl. Signs of life returning to the dark forest. *At las'. A new wee princess mus' be comin'.* He began to dance a little jig. *Alfred shud be pleased.*

CHAPTER THREE

The rustle of wings, and a sharp head-butt, brought Hatchet back to the present. "Wake up, you fool. If you ever hope to have that foot returned to normal, you need to help me find my master. I have searched the world over, and I cannot find even a trace of him. Have you any idea of where he has gone?

"The war appears to be over, but I am not certain, at this moment, who has won. There is no doubt in my mind that my beloved has conquered the enemy. But until I find him, I cannot say for certain. If anyone has harmed one hair of his head, they shall answer to me." She spat out her contempt, and a hot coal rolled over and nudged Hatchet's afflicted ankle.

Hatchet grimaced and shifted his position . . . away from the hot, burning coal. "Oi was no' asleep. Oi was jest restin' me eyes, fer a moment. Tha' is all."

"Asleep, or not, it is of no consequence. You were snoring, and your eyes have been closed for as long as I have been here. I waited as long as I could, but it seemed you would never awaken. Where is my master's book? Do you still have it?"

"Why?" Hatchet stared suspiciously at the huge black dragon. "It be safe."

"Safe? With you? Your ignorance offends me greatly. You know nothing of the book's power, or how to use it. However, safe, or not, I need it. Perhaps I can find the whereabouts of my beloved in its pages. Give it to me. I need it . . . now!"

"Don' you 'ave yer own magic? Use tha'."

"You *are* a fool. Don't you think if I could, I would? I fear there is another magic about. Perhaps even greater than Alfred's, 'though I doubt it. My beloved is the most powerful of all wizards and is unconquerable. But still I worry. Now tell me, where is the book?" She glared at the outlaw and lowered her massive snout to within an inch of his nose, her flashing eyes meeting his terrified orbs. He shifted once again . . . away from those powerful wings, that fiery breath.

"Don' get yer scales in a bind. Oi got it roight 'ere." He raised his right hip and brought out Sirena's Book of Spells.

Maggie, the great black dragon, snatched the book from Hatchet's hands and said, "Thank you. Count your lucky stars you are not a pile of cinders lying on a heap amongst the rubble. Try me again, and I may decide I can do this by myself, and a pile of cinders you may yet become.

"However, if I do find you useful, when I find my beloved, I will plead your case before him, and you may indeed be healed." She glanced toward his afflicted foot and frowned. "It does look nasty, doesn't it?" She sneered. "Does it hurt much? Good. Then I will expect your full cooperation in finding our master."

"'e be no master o' mine."

"Of course, he is. And the sooner you get used to it, the happier you will be. Now, let us look at the book. Perhaps we shall find a clue as to his whereabouts."

"Can ye read it?"

"Of course. Any fool should be able to read it, it's simple enough. It's just a matter of finding the right page . . . the right spell." Maggie stared at the stricken Hatchet, and sighed. "I didn't mean *you* are the fool. Well maybe I did, but I apologize, if it will make you feel any better. Now, where did you find the spell when you first brought him back . . . from the island?"

Hatchet stared at the dragon. "'ow did ye know about tha'?"

Maggie sighed. "My beloved told me everything . . . including your paltry attempt to kill the children in the

Egyptian cave, your failure at protecting him in the mines, and your weakness toward the girl child . . . what was her name? Ah, yes, the talker . . . Sarah, wasn't it? You liked her, I understand. Would you have chosen her over our master? Hmmm. Now that's a thought. No wonder he never trusted you."

The dragon's words stung, but he smiled softly inside at the thought of the little girl, even if she did stomp on his bad foot.

She was just frightened is all, but she was my only friend . . . or had been at one time. She had trusted me, and had things been different . . . .

"You're drifting again," Maggie snapped. "Come back to the present and find me that spell."

Moments later, Hatchet found the familiar spell, and Maggie began to chant.

***

Alfred smiled at Magdalyn as he took his place at the table. He couldn't take his eyes off of her. It was truly a miracle. "I thought I'd never see you again," he murmured.

"Well, my love," she smiled gently. "Here I am, thanks to Merlin and our family. Speaking of family, do you know what time we are to expect them? We don't want a cold dinner, now, do we? Oh, here they come now."

Alfred rose from his chair, and together the two strolled to the front door to welcome the family they loved, but had only recently met. *Family . . . come to dinner.* "It should have always been like this . . . our family together, I mean."

"Alfred, my love, we cannot dwell in the past, but in the present, as we look forward to the future. Look, here come our grandchildren now."

"Is Robert with them?" Alfred squinted, his hand over his eyes.

"Yes, my love, but quite a ways back. The children are running, but Robert is holding back . . . with Harriet. Oh, dear, I do think they may have a little surprise for us." She clapped her hands. "How wonderful."

***

"Excellent, as usual, Mother."

"I'm glad you liked it, Robert, and it's good to see *you* eating well, Harriet, my dear. It's been some time since you two have visited, and you look radiant. When is the blessed event?"

"Blessed event?" Alfred looked confused. "What blessed event?"

Robert leaned across the table. "You're going to be a grandfather again, Father. What do you think about that?"

Alfred rose and walked slowly to his daughter-in-law.

Taking her hands in his, he gazed, with wonder, into her eyes and asked, "Is this true, my dear? Am I about to become a grandpa again?" At the expression in her eyes, and her tiny smile of joy, he began to whoop. "Blessed be the God of Heaven," he shouted. "He has given me another chance. So," he turned toward Robert, "when is the blessed event? And is it a boy or a girl? If it's a boy, I know a perfectly good name, and if it's a girl," he glanced at his wife, smiling softly, "I know an ever better one."

"We don't know yet, but as soon as we do, we'll let you know. And Father, we have been talking, and if we have a boy, we will be naming him Alfred Robert, and if it's a girl," he turned toward his mother, "Magdalyn is a beautiful name. Don't you think?"

In answer, Alfred ran to his wife, picked her up, and whirled her around the room.

"Alfred, put me down," she squealed. And he did, collapsing onto the floor, a startled expression on his face.

"Father, what's the matter?"

"Alfred, you're fading. Alfred!"

"Hold me, tightly, all of you. I am being pulled . . . away."

Magdalyn grabbed onto her husband as Robert and the children leaped forward and attached themselves to his arms and legs, Harriet at his head.

"Keep holding," Alfred shouted, "or I am lost."

Moments later, the exhausted family finally relaxed their hold as Alfred panted on the wooden slat floor. Finally attempting to rise, he smiled at his family. "My, that was a close one."

"Father, what are you talking about? What just happened?"

Alfred sat up. "I have been through this before. Hatchet is calling me with a spell from the Magic Book of Spells. Thank you for holding me. I cannot go . . . . I must stay with those I love."

"Hey, Grandpa," Sure-shot jumped in "That's a no-brainer. You couldn't leave anyway. There's a spell on this painting, remember. You can't leave here."

"'Tis but true. The magic on this painting is powerful, but the magic of a dragon can be even more powerful."

"Maggie? Do you think she's helping Hatchet?"

"Without a doubt. But I cannot go." Alfred smiled up at his love. "I will never leave you again. I promise." But his heart hurt as he remembered the strength of the pull. Could he resist the pull? Or would the old magic overpower his will? Dragon magic along with dragon determination was hard to resist. "Robert, my son, you must call on Merlin.

Only he has the power to keep me here . . . with those I love."

***

"It's no' workin'," grumbled Hatchet.

"Of course, it is," Maggie snapped. "You're just not trying hard enough. I felt his presence. We almost had him. We must try again."

"I canno'. Per'aps lat'r, after oi've rested a bit."

"We cannot wait. My beloved was almost in our hands. We cannot give up now."

"Thar be a most powerful force attendin' 'im. We'll not be calling 'im successfulike now."

"Perhaps you're right. If there *are* powerful forces preventing him from returning, we could tear him apart . . . if we are not careful. That will never do. We must think on this. We must find out where he has been taken captive and rescue him, at our own peril, if necessary. Come, we must think hard on this. He must be found and rescued before it is too late. Give me the book. I shall attempt to find him, and then we can try again. The book . . . Hatchet. Do not forget, your healing also depends on the return of your master."

"He be no' me master." Hatchet grumbled, but nevertheless handed the book of spells over to the dragon. "Here, ye black devil. Do wit' it as ye wish. Jest make sure me fut is healed, and ye kin 'ave the blasted book."

Maggie took the book firmly in her mouth, and flew away. Perhaps someone more knowledgeable could help her in her quest for Alfred's return. And perhaps not, but it was worth a try. She flew off to find her father, the dragon king.

CHAPTER FOUR

Maggie lightly touched down at the mouth of the royal cave and laid the book of magic at her feet. "What are you doing here?" she sneered at the large green dragon protecting the entrance to the dragon throne room.

"I am protecting our father from unnecessary intrusion," Ellie answered with a guarded smile. "To what delight have you come. We have not seen you in some time. Our father, the king, has asked about you on occasion."

"You should know, your majesty," spat the black dragon. "You seem to make it your business to know everything about everything . . . these days."

"Now, Maggie, dear," soothed Ellie, "you know you are always welcome here. This is your home as much as it is mine."

"Your generosity is unprecedented. Were *I* queen, instead of you, I would not be so charming. It could lead to your undoing . . . if you know what I mean." She smiled malevolently. "However, as you say, he is *our* father, and I have need to speak with him . . . urgently.

"Does this have anything to do with Alfred? You will not find him, you know. I do not mean to be unkind, but he is happy now . . . with his true family . . . his human family."

"You know naught of what you speak. I am his family—his only true family."

"My dear sister, Father is not well, so I cannot allow you to disturb him. However, should you truly wish to know where Alfred is, to see him with your own eyes, perhaps I can remedy that."

"You?! What right do you have to show me anything? Only the highest royals have . . . that . . . ability." Maggie stared intently at her sister, for just a moment, her eyes flashing as a burst of anger flooded her being. "So, you have stolen my birthright, and you are now queen?"

"I'm sorry, Maggie. I had nothing to do with it. Father is very old, and he thought I would do the best job to rule the kingdom. He felt you were just a bit . . . how can I say this gently enough? Okay." Ellie took a deep breath. "He thought your temperament a bit too—"

"My temperament? My temperament is perfect to rule, and as the elder, it is my birthright. You had no right to accept the throne in my absence. I must speak to Father immediately. Get out of my way."

Maggie attempted to push by Ellie, but gasped as her sister was joined by several huge dragons, and the queen mother herself.

"I'm so sorry, Maggie, my dear," the queen mother spoke softly and with great love for this first born. "But your father has chosen, and not even I could persuade him to change his mind. However, you will be glad to know that Ellie makes a wonderful, and just, queen. It seems *she* is most suited for the job. I'm so sorry, dear, but your father has spoken, and we dare not challenge his decision. Listen to Ellie, dear. She could do a lot for you, if you were so inclined to work *with* her instead of against her."

*Neve*r. Maggie frowned, but bit her tongue, lest she say something that would get her banished . . . forever. She straightened her shoulders, folded her wings close to her side in seeming subjugation, and bowed low to her sister. Through gritted teeth, she continued. "My sister, my queen. If you would indeed be so kind as to show me the whereabouts of Alfred, I would be . . . eternally . . . grateful." *Ugh . . . I got it out, no matter how distasteful, but unfortunately, I need her help.*

"Maggie, Maggie, what good would it do? Seeing him happy with his family will only serve to hurt you. I would rather you not be hurt, but if you insist, I will show you your

Alfred."

"*I* am his family, and he *will* return to me. No one can make him happier than I. Now show me my beloved."

Ellie sighed. "As you wish, my sister, but don't say I didn't warn you. Come with me."

The dragon guards parted, allowing the sisters passage, but still kept a close watch on the two. Within moments they entered the inner sanctum, and Maggie watched the projection on the flat wall of the cave.

"No, no . . . . Alfred . . . come back to me," she cried, but her heart felt as lead, and she mourned her loss. "Who is that woman?" she hissed. "I know the others. His ungrateful son, and that snip of a boy, but who are the others?"

"Maggie, dear," Ellie began, as gently as she could. "The white-haired woman is his wife, after whom you were named. Magdalyn is her name. The others are his son, as you know, his son's wife, and his grandchildren. It appears another grandchild is on the way as well."

"No, no! He belongs to me! I shall win him back, and I shall steal this new grandchild as well. He will learn to love me again. I will be his favorite, and I will have the child." She turned and began to stalk toward the cave entrance.

"Maggie, no! I know how you feel, but he is happy now. Is that not what you want . . . his happiness? Why not

let him live in peace, in his old age, with the family he loves
. . . and who obviously love him?"

Maggie briefly turned back to her sister and snarled.
"They are but temporary. I know he loves me best. He told
me so, and our love will conquer all. He will be mine again,
and no one, not even you, can stop us from being together.
Good-bye, sister, dear, my so-called queen. And don't get
in my way, if you know what's good for you."

Ellie watched sadly as Maggie flew off. *You are
powerful, Maggie, but you cannot do this by yourself. You
will not prevail, but will only be hurt worse than you
already are.* Turning to her mother, she said. "Please look
after Father. I must go to Robert. He must be advised of this
current situation."

"As you say, my dear, but please be careful. Your sister
may indeed attempt harm, and I don't want to lose both of
my daughters. Blessings on your quest, my . . . daughter
queen. I await your safe return."

Ellie smiled and hugged her mother as best she could
and turned to leave. "Thank you, Mother. I will return as
soon as I am able. Should Maggie return home, I leave it to
your discretion as to what to tell her of my whereabouts.
Good-bye, Mother. I'll be back as soon as I can." With that
said, Ellie took to the skies to find her beloved Robert, and

the family. They must be warned at once.

***

"A close call, I'd say." Merlin stroked his long white beard and sighed. "It shouldn't have happened. Someone out there must be very powerful indeed. I will have to double up on the spell of protection on this painting. You say you think Hatchet has an accomplice, and they are putting the come hither on Alfred?"

"Not a doubt in my mind. Maggie, Ellie's sister, thinks of Alfred as her lover, and will stop at nothing to have him returned to her."

"Maggie? Ellie? Ah yes, the dragon sisters. Two more different family members I have a hard time in perceiving . . . unless you count Arthur and Morgana . . . but then again, they, also, were half siblings. Hmmmm. Something to think about."

"You see, Merlin, my father saved Maggie's life, and in doing so he garnered her absolute loyalty. He even named her after my mother, his one true love he thought he had lost forever. I'm not sure whether Maggie knows my father has been returned to the love of his life, but if she is aware, things are likely to become mighty tense around here. She fancies herself in love with him."

"Ah, yes, that could be a problem." He continued to

stroke his beard, his mind far away. "Well, this is going to take some thought, but whatever we do, we cannot let Alfred out of our sight, not even for a moment. I will upgrade the spell on the painting, but dragon magic can be fiercely strong."

Magdalyn gripped her husband's arm. "If it's a fight she wants, a fight she will get. There is no magic so powerful as the love a woman has for her husband. She's had him long enough.

He belongs to me and will always belong to me."

"Well said, Mother. "

"Don't worry, Grandma. I know Grandpa, and he would never leave us for anything. Not even a pet dragon."

"Sure-shot, my son," Alfred broke in, "Maggie was not simply a pet, but at the time, she was my best friend, the epitome of your grandmother. I poured the love I felt for your grandmother into that dragon, not knowing I would ever have the chance to partake of your grandmother's love again. We must be gentle with Maggie, for I am certain she means us no harm." He smiled with great tenderness at his wife. "I love you most dearly, my love, but I'm afraid Maggie considers herself to be you, in her own dragon way."

"I understand, my darling, but a dragon's love does not

compare with mine. But still we must be careful."

"Then it's settled. I will double the spell on the painting, and you," he gestured around the room, "will protect him from the inside. I think it might be best if all of you were to reside here for the time being – for the protection of you all, you see. I must go. I will return as soon as I can. In the meantime, don't do anything foolish. Such as seek out this dragon and try to talk some sense into her. You will only serve to strengthen her resolve. Good-bye, for now. I shall return as soon as I am able. However, should you need me, please don't hesitate to send a nine-one-one." He grinned. "I'm getting pretty good at this jargon. But I must go. Be safe. Until we meet again." And he was gone.

* * *

Maggie watched, from the safety of the castle painting, the elderly wizard as he chanted a spell over a lovely pristine painting on the far wall. Her heart began to beat faster. *Alfred? Is that you?* But . . . no . . . . The wizard turned, and although there was some resemblance, this man was not Alfred. She attempted to push her snout into the great room but was unsuccessful.

The strange wizard casually strolled toward the castle painting and stared at the huge black dragon. "Maggie, is it?

So, you have found me. I can see you are indeed beautiful. No wonder Alfred named you after his one true love. Give it up, Maggie. Alfred is where he belongs, and you will never be able to separate him from his only true love . . . his wife, Magdalyn.

"By the way, each of the paintings have been sealed, so any attempt you may seek to enter this room will be futile. Go home, Maggie. Alfred is where he belongs . . . with his family." He smiled a friendly smile at the dragon, but she took it as a challenge and bared her teeth. Taking a deep breath, the dragon hissed at the somewhat familiar wizard, and he jumped backward. The painting now had a circular burn mark from the inside of the painting.

"Nice try, Maggie, but as you can see, the magic holds. Go home, now. Find someone more of your own species to love and leave Alfred alone." Muttering a few words, he resealed the painting, turned and left, his stomach in knots. *She is far more powerful than I had at first thought. She should not have been able to singe the painting.*

Maggie watched as the old wizard left, and once more attempted to thrust her snout through the painting, but to no avail. Resolute, she turned and stretched her wings. *Another day, another time. Hatchet, I'm coming home. We are going to need to do this thing together.* Lifting her wings, she began to fly, back where a frustrated Hatchet waited her return.

Merlin sighed a great sigh of relief, as he watched her take flight. A temporary respite, if that. He shivered inside. She could be a formidable opponent. She would bear watching. "Professor," he shouted. "I have need of your services. Come quickly."

But all was silent in the great room.

CHAPTER FIVE

Ellie soared above the dense forest, her dragon eyes scanning the countryside. To her left a tiny creature stood at the threshold of the great room entrance, and she panicked for just a moment. *Maggie . . . how did she find this place? This is not good. I must warn Robert.*

As quietly as she could, she drifted to the ground, some distance from her sister. Camouflaging with the trees, she made her way to the entrance to the great room and listened at the conversation taking place. *Oh, Maggie, will you never learn?*

She watched as the wizard, Merlin, mouthed some words and left. She watched as Maggie tried once again to force her head through the portal to no success. She watched as her sister, in disgust, hissed at the threshold, then stretched her mighty wings and flew off.

Had Maggie been less intent on finding and rescuing Alfred, she may have noticed her sister lurking in the shadows, but she was not, so she had no idea Ellie was there to speak to Alfred's son, Robert.

* * *

Ellie was of mixed emotions. She hurt for her sister, but she could not allow Maggie the pleasure of destroying Robert's family, if indeed that were possible. She watched as Maggie took to the sky before venturing to the portal entrance, herself.

She stared, for just a moment, at the circular burn mark barely visible to the dragon eye, and when great dragon tears fell from those eyes, she took them and spread them upon the mark. Gone, and as good as if it had never been there at all.

It may have been an accidental finding on Maggie's part, and if it was, it was imperative she not be able to find the threshold so easily should she try again. And Ellie knew she would try . . . again . . . and again . . . as often as it took to return to the human she loved. *But he does not belong to you, Maggie, dear. He belongs to another. You have no rights here.*

She began to call her own human friend. *Robert . . . Robert . . . come to the great room. We need to talk.* Yes, talk they must do . . . formulate a plan. Robert and his family must be warned. Chaos was about to erupt.

* * *

"Hatchet! Hatchet! Wake up! I have discovered the whereabouts of our master."

"Oi'm no' asleepin'. Oi'm contemplatin' me book."

"Well, my dear, while you have been simply contemplating, I have found where he is being kept prisoner. A strange new wizard has locked him in a painting and has forbidden me access. I cannot do it alone, so, you are going to need to help me get through the barrier."

"Me? What kin oi' do, tha' ye canno'?"

Maggie shuddered. "First of all, you can learn to speak proper, and then to read. It may take some time, a lot of time," she muttered, "but with my help you should soon become, if not fluent, at least somewhat adequate. Besides, Alfred is much more likely to heal you if he considers you worthy of healing, and that means you simply must learn to speak properly. And you must learn to read. It will be much easier to call him back if we both work intelligently on the process. As the old saying goes, 'two heads are better than one.' Although, in this case, I wonder," she murmured. "Nevertheless, it is imperative we work together to remedy our current situation and rescue my beloved."

"Wat did this strange wizard tell ye?"

"It really doesn't matter, but if you insist, he said that Alfred is happy with his family, including a 'wife' long dead. Certainly, he cannot desire a dead woman over me."

"But wat if she be made alive, again. A wife alive is worth more than a thousan' dragons, oi' would say."

"Nobody asked you," she spat, another hot coal rolling toward Hatchet's affected foot.

Hatchet stomped out the glowing coal and glared at the dragon. "If ye be needin' me 'elp, then don' be doin' tha'."

"Sorry, but if we are going to work together to bring him back, I need a little more help, and a lot less talk." Maggie glared once again at Hatchet, and then softened. *Perhaps, if I could teach him some manners, as well as to read and speak properly, we could get along better. In any case, if the master could put up with him, perhaps he isn't so bad after all.*

* * *

Robert startled, jumping inside as a familiar voice began to call his name. Scooting back his chair, he mumbled something incoherent to those around him.

"What's the matter, Dad? Are you okay?"

Robert grimaced. He had forgotten how in tune he and Sure-shot had become. "I'm fine," he smiled. "I just need to excuse myself for a few minutes."

"Well, my son," interjected Alfred. "If it's the privy you'll be needing, it's—"

"No, that's alright. I just need a bit of fresh air."

Magdalyn rose, and quickly rushed to her son's side, placing the back of her hand against his forehead. "Are you certain, dear? You look a bit pale."

His mother's concern touched him, but he answered, "I'm just fine." He took her hand in his and patted it gently. "There's no need to worry your pretty head about anything. As I said, I'm just fine.

"Now, look what you've done. Harriet's all upset. And with the new baby, and all, we can't have Harriet upset, now can we. Besides, there is absolutely nothing wrong with me. I'm as healthy as a . . . a . . . dragon." He grinned, showing pearly white teeth.

"Um, Dad? I think you're needed . . . in the great room? I think someone's calling you. I'll take care of Mom and Grandma. You go see what Ellie wants. I'm sure it's probably really important."

Alfred scooched back in his chair. "Do you think I should come along, Robert? I may be needed."

"No!" said Robert, a little too quickly. "You need to take care of the women and the children. You know what almost happened. If Ellie *is* calling me, it might have something to do with Maggie, and we can't take any chances where that dragon is concerned." He frowned as Alfred stood in protest.

The cabin door flew open and Merlin peered into the room. "Oh . . . hello. Am I missing something? Has anyone seen the professor? I really need to find the professor."

"Come in, Merlin. Have a seat, and tell us what's going on." Alfred's voice was friendly, but firm.

"Um, yes," he hedged, quietly entering the cabin. "But I really do need to find Professor Hawthorn. Perhaps later."

Alfred raised a hand and the door slammed shut. "Now, would be a good time."

Merlin glanced toward Robert. "I think you're being called."

"Yes," Robert swallowed. "I really should be on my way."

"I think not," Alfred said stubbornly. "You two know something, and if it involves me, I feel I have the right to know."

"Yes," broke in Harriet, rising and standing by her mother-in-law, both women with their arms crossed over their chests. "Tell all, Robert . . . Merlin, unless you want a mutiny on your hands."

Merlin glanced toward Robert, and the younger man shrugged and slightly nodded his approval.

"Sit down, everyone." Merlin sighed. "Ellie is in the castle picture to warn Robert that Maggie has tried to enter the great-room, searching for the one she calls her beloved - Alfred, here. She says she will stop at nothing to get him back. I fear she means to do bodily harm to anyone who stands in her way, and that includes our lovely Magdalyn."

He nodded toward his hostess.

Magdalyn stood straight and tall. "If it's war she wants, then war she'll get. I've learned a thing or two through the years, and no dragon is going to deprive me of my husband. No one," she emphasized, stabbing at the air with her index finger. "Besides," she murmured, "I have the best five wizards in the country to defend me. And you might be surprised, I just might have a little dragon magic in me, as well." At the startled looks from her family, she continued. "Well, how do you think I was able to retrieve that ring." She nodded at Merlin's hand.

"You mean; you knew about the powers of the ring when you gave it to me?" Alfred eyes grew wide.

"Of course, my love. I'd played with it for years. That's why I wanted it so badly. I knew of its power, but I also knew only a great wizard could fully utilize that power." She softened. "And when you came into my life, I knew that you were the one destined for the ring, and our children and grandchildren as well. The only thing I did not know was that the original owner was Merlin. But things worked out quite well, don't you think?"

"Indubitably!" Merlin slapped his leg in glee. "I knew I left my ring in good hands. I just didn't know whose hands they were. Congratulations, my dear. No wonder the magic is so strong in your family. I should have known." He laughed, then turned to Robert. "Robert, you must go to Ellie. We must form a plan."

"Yes, Robert," Harriet smiled and took her husband's arm. "We must hurry. Ellie is calling to us."

"Us?" Robert raised his eyebrows.

"Of course. You don't think I'd let you go alone, do you?"

"Grandma, can you take care of Amanda Joy? We've got work to do."

"Of course, Harold . . . I mean . . . Sure-shot." She smiled affectionately at her grandson as she picked up the tiny girl.

"Wanna go. Me wanna go . . . too," Amanda Joy burbled as she stretched toward her mother.

"Not this time, Pumpkin," soothed Robert. "We need you to take care of your grandparents. Can you do that for us? Keep Grandpa safe from the big mean dragon, and Grandma, too?"

Amanda Joy thought for a moment and then grinned.

"Yes, Daddy. Me a big girl now."

"Yes, you are, and Daddy and Mommy are so proud of you." He gave his daughter a fierce hug before turning and heading for the door. "We'll be right back. Watch out for Grandpa. We don't know how powerful Maggie and Hatchet have become. Love all of you. We'll be back as soon as we can. Be good."

And they were gone.

Merlin pulled up a chair and leaned casually on the table where Robert had once sat. He motioned for Magdalyn to have a seat. "Madam, we need to talk."

"About what?" she asked demurely, setting her granddaughter onto the floor to play, and taking a seat.

He stared at Magdalyn and smiled. "As if you didn't know."

Amanda Joy toddled over to Merlin and climbed into his lap. Taking the white bearded face in her pudgy little hands, she asked, "Yes, Unca Merl. 'bout what?"

He held up his hand. The orange stone sparkled with glee.

Amanda Joy squealed with delight, reaching for the sparkly object.

Merlin moved his hand slightly, and murmured, "About what, indeed, my dear girl?"

CHAPTER SIX

"Ungh. Why do I even put up with you? You don't appear to be completely stupid, but maybe I have misjudged your potential." Maggie sneered at Hatchet as he attempted to recite the alphabet. "Are you an idiot, Hatchet? Do you have any intelligence at all, or am I just wasting my time?"

"Oi'm smart enough t' know w'en Oi'm wanted and w'en Oi'm not, thank ye."

"What do you mean by that remark?" Maggie hissed in anger. "Everyone wants me," she huffed. "Everyone loves me."

"Figger it out, ifin yer so smart."

"I could burn you to a cinder with one breath, if I wished. I would show some respect, if I were you." She spat another small coal in the outlaw's direction and tossed her head in the air at his seeming lack of response.

Hatchet rose, and gathered up his belongings, including his precious book of spells. "So long. 'ave a nice life."

Perplexed, and somewhat confused, Maggie stretched out one massive wing blocking Hatchet's pathway. "And where do you think you're going . . . sir?" she crooned, with a side of nasty temper. "And where are you taking Alfred's book?"

"Oi be goin' 'ome, where oi'm bein' appreciated. An oi'm takin' me book wit' me."

"The book is not yours. It is Alfred's, and since only I can read it, as it should be read, the book should come to me. Give it to me . . . now . . . and then if you must be on your way, so be it. I shall bring him back myself." She held out a dragon hand, demanding the book of spells.

"No' on yer dragon life. Th' book belongs t' me. I found it. I'm keepin' it." He stuck the book under his tunic.

Maggie stared at the outlaw her eyes open wide. "What did you say?"

"I said, I'm keepin' it. An' that's that!"

"Oh, Hatchet. Did you just hear yourself? You said 'I'm' instead of Oi'm." She grabbed him in her huge dragon arms. "I guess there's hope for you after all." She planted a dragon kiss on the top of his head, set him back down on the pathway, and began to pace the small clearing. "This is wonderful . . . wonderful. Now we can really get down to business. But not here. Too many distractions." She paused before continuing. "Hatchet, my dear! We're going home, back to the island. "

"W'at? And 'ow are we supposed t' git there. Fly?"

"Exactly."

"No, no, no, no, no. Oi, er, I, canno fly. No, no, no, no, no." He turned and began to hurry down the path as best his lame foot would let him.

"Yes, yes, yes, yes, yes," Maggie purred, as she snatched up the fleeing outlaw, and stretched her mighty wings. Takeoff was a bit slow with the added burden of a struggling human, shrieking in her ear. "Relax, Hatchet. It will make it easier on the both of us. Close your eyes and relax."

"I canno' relax. Put me down."

"Hatchet," Maggie sighed. "You have a choice - I will grant you that. I can carry you in my arms, though they may be a bit weakened by your weight, or you can do as Alfred used to love to do – you can ride on my back, which would really be better for both of us . . . if you know what I mean. But one way or the other, we are going to the island, and together we will have victory over those puny humans. Your choice, my dear. My back . . . or my arms." She pretended to loosen her grip as Hatchet shrieked –

"Don't drop me. I'll ride on yer back, if tha's w'at it tikes. Jest don't drop me."

"As you wish." She began to drift toward the earth.

"And Hatchet? You are already beginning to speak better. I'm proud of you. We will certainly work out for the best. She touched the ground and spread out one massive wing. "Climb aboard," she sang, but at Hatchet's hesitation snapped, "Unless you would like to be carried . . . like a baby . . . and possibly dropped in the middle of the ocean . . . and—"

She grinned, as a terrified Hatchet scrambled up her wing and onto her back, securing his feet and knees in her wing sockets, and laying forward upon her brawny back, his arms clutching her thick neck.

"Not so tight, rider, or we both might end up in the water."

Hatchet loosened his grip, just a bit, but kept his eyes squeezed tightly shut, until they were well on their way. At last he began to relax, a tad, and ventured a peek at the landscape zipping by. *Whoa . . . t'is beautiful up here.* He gingerly sat up a bit straighter and gave a gentle pat on the smooth black neck.

Maggie smiled to herself. *Hatchet isn't so bad. I could get used to this.* And on they flew toward their island home.

CHAPTER SEVEN

Maggie sprawled on the nursery floor, sighing deeply. Fine shells littered the cavern, and she scraped them up, crushing them as she went, gathering them into a rough, but somewhat pleasant nest. She missed her charges, but they had been *misled* into following Ellie, who sometimes was not dragon-like at all. *A kind and gentle spirit Father thinks more suited to be queen than I, his first born. How could he? Have I not always and forever done his bidding. But yet he chose **her** . . . a more even temperament, he said.*

She snarled in her semi-sleep. *I have an even temperament, and if he would only have listened, he would have seen that I, Maggie, am much more suited to be queen, than my human-loving sister.* A dragon tear slipped from her eye, and she wondered what Hatchet was up to, now, seemingly her only friend, of sorts.

For three weeks, now, they had been on the island, but not much progress had been made. It is true Hatchet had attempted to study, to learn to read and write, but he seemed restless, and took long walks on their side of the mountain.

He seemed lonely, and unsure of himself. *How could he be lonely? He has me, doesn't he.* She sighed again, fidgeting in her slumber.

Humph, she grunted. *Perhaps he needs human companionship. I don't know why, but that seems to be the way humans do things. We can't seem to free Alfred, but perhaps the little girl . . . the mouthy one. He seems quite taken with her. Yes, I will call the girl. We can use her for ransom, if need be, or as a trade-off for my beloved Alfred. In the meantime, perhaps she can get Hatchet out of his funk, as the humans call it. Now what was her name? Oh, yes. Sarah. Sarah, the . . . mouthy one . . . the . . .talker. Later . . . I'll call . . . her . . . later . . . .* She smiled. At last she had a plan. And she fell fast asleep.

* * *

Sarah sat in the kennel, the little dog, Belle, and her puppies snuggled in her lap. Belle was Belinda's dog, but she didn't seem to have much time for her, as of late, so Sarah took over, brushing and petting, and loving the little dogs. She jumped as a sudden breeze wafted around her, and she wondered where it came from. A slight growl rose from Belle's throat, and she snuggled deeper in the little girl's lap.

Sarah . . . Sarah . . . she heard in her mind. *We need*

you, Sarah.

"Did you hear something?" she asked the little dog, scratching her behind her ears. But the little dog just continued her low-pitched growl, occasionally planting a quick doggy kiss on her companion. "Oh, well, I guess not. But it sounded . . . so . . . real. Listen. There it goes again. Are you sure you can't hear it? It's . . . telling me . . . to go to . . . the . . . great room . but . . . we're not . . . supposed . . .to go . . . to the great room."

As if in a trance the little girl set the puppies gently on the ground, rose, and headed toward the big house. Belle jumped up and grabbed the cuff of her pants, and began to pull, growling as she held on.

Sarah paused just long enough to untangle the tiny teeth from her jeans, and began to run toward the house, Belle at her heels, barking all the way. *Don't go*, she seemed to say. *Stay with me where you'll be safe.*

But the little girl was beyond hearing as she raced toward the big house and the great room door. No one would know she had even been there. She would just stay a little while, just until she found the answer to her strange calling.

She reached the front door in record time, carefully slipping through, and shutting the door behind her, leaving

Belle stranded on the porch, barking and barking, and barking, calling anyone to rush to Sarah's rescue. But, no one came.

Sarah opened the great room door, and peered in. Strange . . . the door is unlocked . . . it's . . . never unlocked. Slowly shutting the heavy door, she sauntered toward the painting at the back of the room. A huge black dragon smiled at her there.

* * *

Alfred jumped and stood, trembling as he faced the door.

"Alfred?" asked Magdalyn dropping her mending in the large basket at her side. "What's wrong? She grabbed his sleeve. "Alfred, tell me what's wrong. Now!"

"The child. I must go to her. She's in danger. Her life may be at stake."

"What child?" Magdalyn asked, panic in her voice.

"Sarah. She is in the great room. Maggie has called her, and I'm sure she is up to no good."

"Sarah? Maggie? Oh, my Lord. Please, God, save the child."

Alfred, with Magdalyn in close pursuit began to run toward the painting entrance. "Sarah," they screamed. "Don't listen to Maggie. Come back."

But Sarah was beyond hearing.

The huge black dragon smiled sweetly at the little girl. "Come child, quickly" she said. "A friend of yours needs you. Do you remember Hatchet? Ah, yes, I see that you do. Well, child, Hatchet is having some difficulties in his new life, and longs for his only friend to come to his aid. I am afraid that he may die, if you refuse to come.

"Please, my child, he needs you. Come with me. I will take you to him. Do not be afraid. I mean you no harm, but I have become concerned about our mutual friend, as he seems very down, and may not be able to pull himself out of his despair . . . without your help. I mean. Will you come and care for an old friend? He needs you, and as soon as he is well, I will return you to your present home. I promise."

"But . . ." *Hatchet is an outlaw. And everybody says he cannot be trusted. But he did save my life. He wouldn't let anything happen to me. He is my friend. If he's sick, and if he needs me, maybe I should go.* She stepped toward the panting.

"No, no, don't go. She can't be trusted," screamed the air in the painting. "Sarah, turn around. Look at me." Alfred coaxed. "Come back."

Maggie softened as she spotted her beloved in the painting on the far wall, her dragon heart soaring with love, and almost relented. But the woman clinging to his arm, that woman he called wife, hardened her soul, and she reached out a hand for the small child. "Come," she smiled, but grimaced when her hand touched the barrier. "Drat, I can't get through," she muttered.

Alfred breathed a sigh of relief and patted his wife's hand. "We forgot. Merlin's spell. She cannot enter the great room. Sarah, come back. Now."

But Sarah could neither see, nor hear their pleas. The voice of the dragon was too strong in her mind. She stood in front of the painting and said, "Do you promise you won't hurt me, and will bring me back when I want to come back?"

"Of course, my darling child. I promise a dragon promise, and a dragon promise is sacred. You will be safe, and as soon as Hatchet is well, I will bring you back. Are we in agreement?"

"O-okay. But you have to keep your promise, or Merlin will cook your hide big time."

"Merlin? Who is this Merlin? But don't worry, you will be safe. Now hurry. Come to me, for I cannot come to you. Hurry, Hatchet needs you. Give me your hand, child."

Obediently, Sarah walked up to the painting, and extended her hand.

"Put your hand through the painting," Maggie coaxed,

"and I will help you through. Good girl. You're almost here." She gripped the child's hand and roughly pulled her through the painting and onto the castle path. "There, isn't that much better? Well, child, we must be on our way. We are needed."

Sarah glanced toward the great room, just as the door flew open, and Merlin and Aunt Gwenny, with a worried, barking, Belle, barreled through. "Wait," she cried. "I have to say good-bye to my friends."

"It's too late," Maggie shrieked, grabbing the child and extending her wings. Moments later the two were in the air, and Sarah was clinging to the dragon as if her life depended on it. As indeed it might very well be.

With wand extended Merlin ran to the painting, muttering a few words to dissipate the spell. Stepping through the painting and onto the path, he searched the skies, but the dragon and the little girl could not be found.

"This is not good," he muttered. "This is certainly not good. I must speak to Bee, immediately. We must come up with a plan, yes, we certainly must." He exited the painting, and with Gwenny by his side, rushed to tell the mother queen, that her granddaughter had been stolen. "Lord God, great Creator," he prayed, "be merciful and protect the child. Reveal to us her whereabouts, so that she may be recovered."

Bee Lewis swept through the great room door, and frowned. "What is going on in here? This racket is enough to wake the dead."

Aunt Gwenny took both of her best friend's hands in her own, and with tears in her eyes, said. "Bee, dear. We have a problem. Sit down, dear. We have bad news. We were on our way to find you, and . . . ."

Bee struggled out of Gwenny's hands, tightly gripped her best friend's upper arms, and said, with panic in her voice, "What bad news? What are you talking about? And why is everyone in the great room? And why is Magdalyn sobbing? What's going on here?"

"My dear girl," Merlin said softly, bowing his head slightly. "Your Majesty . . . I'm so sorry. Our little Sarah has been stolen . . . by Maggie. We don't know where she has taken her, but we must find and rescue her, before something dire takes place."

Bee clutched her chest, and gasped. "Sarah, my precious Sarah, is gone. We must find her. What are we going to do?"

"The first thing we must do," Alfred called from the painting, "is not to panic. I'm certain Maggie will not hurt the child, but I am just as certain, that she needs Sarah . . .

for some purpose of which we do not know. I say we check out Dragon Island, and the island where I was kept captive. She will consider it familiar and safe. And if Hatchet is with her, our island would be the perfect place to hide out. Merlin, you must release me from the painting, for we will not find her without my assistance."

"I'm sorry, Alfred," Merlin sympathized, "but it would be dangerous to remove the spell. She may be willing to trade Sarah, for you, but then she may not. You could lose everything you know and love. If you should refuse her . . . You know the old saying 'a woman scorned.' Well a dragon scorned can do a lot more damage . . . to you, but mostly to Magdalyn. Are you willing to take a chance with her life?

"Merlin?" Magdalyn broke in, "I am not afraid of Maggie. She has no idea who and what she is up against. I'm with Alfred. Please release us both from the painting. If my life is required for that little girl, so be it, but I don't see that happening. I am a lot stronger than you might think . . . and wiser . . . and powerful . . . and . . . ."

"All right, I get the picture. But please be careful, and don't do anything foolish. Promise me."

"We will do our best." Alfred smiled and put his arms around his wife, who smiled her own agreement."

"If that's all I can get, it will have to do. I admire your

bravery. Let's just hope it doesn't bring you to your own demise. Stand back." With a wave of his hand, and a few muttered words, the spell was broken, and Alfred and Magdalyn were released from the painting, still holding tightly to each other.

"At last, we have returned to the land of the living," Alfred shouted, before becoming entwined in the arms of those about him. "Come," he choked, with moisture in his eyes, "we have a job to do. And we'd best be about it."

Together, they exited the great room. Time was of the essence.

CHAPTER EIGHT

Sarah shivered and drew the thin blanket over her neck and shoulders, her exposed feet twitching with the cold. Hatchet watched her for just a moment, and then sighed, taking his own blanket and covering the little girl from head to toe, taking care to tuck the blanket securely around her small frame.

He found it hard to sleep as the cold wind bit into his own bare skin, goosebumps covering his arms and legs. He didn't like the cold – never had, never would, but the wee bearn needed the warmth more than he, and so he offered all he had.

Sarah turned over and snuggled into Hatchet's chest, grabbing the edge of the blanket and attempting to cover her friend's arm and shoulder.

Hatchet smiled, in spite of the cold. The little girl cared about him, he was certain, and that was why he must protect her, even if it cost him his own life. She was his only true friend.

Maggie scrutinized these two humans, the large and the

small, and rolled her dragon eyes. Just when she thought she knew the outlaw he turned and did something nice for someone. *Oh, bother*, she grunted as she shifted her huge body to the bedrock next to Hatchet and covered both the man and the child with one massive wing. It felt strange, but nice, in a bizarre sort of way.

The man and the child ceased shivering and settled into a deep, restful sleep, warmed by this comfy 'leather' blanket, of sorts. Maggie slept with one eye open, even as she rested. It would never do to be caught unawares, if any of the enemy were about.

The warmth from the human bodies soon lulled her into a dreamlike state, and she drifted off, her huge eye slowly closing, against her will. She blew a quick breath of warm air into Hatchet's hair, and before she could stop herself, fell asleep.

***

Maggie awoke with a start. *Voices . . . human voices . . . in the distance . . . near the cave.* She smiled. Her instincts had been correct, once again. Sleeping on a cold outcropping wasn't her idea of comfort, but since the child had been taken, she knew the first place the enemy would scour would be the cave. But knowing that, she left, for parts unknown, at least to those unfamiliar to the island. *They can explore the cavern to their hearts content, but will find not a single bit of evidence. Nothing . . . nothing at all.*

And then they will leave, and we three can return to the comfort of our cavern home. Only Alfred would be able to tell if someone were occupying the caves, but he is locked in a painting where he cannot get out. She sighed

Her companions stirred, and she pulled them closer. It would not do for the two to awaken while the enemy was so close. The sun, now high in the Heaven's, would not be noticed, as she had placed a spell over the sleeping duo. They would think it still night, and with her dragon ability to hide in plain sight, she was not worried about being found. Should someone glance in their direction, they would see nothing. As long as everyone kept still, no one would ever know.

"Maggie?" Sarah yawned. "I need to go to the bathroom."

"Ung," Maggie muttered. *Not now. Not with the enemy so close.* "Shhh," she whispered. "All in good time. Go back to sleep. It is yet early."

"But, I gotta go now."

"Alright, give me just a moment to figure out the best place for you to go."

"Okay . . . but hurry up. I'm going to split."

Anxiously, Maggie glanced toward the cavern. *The enemy is leaving . . . everyone.* She breathed a sigh of relief.

"Maggie! Please!"

"Um, yes, dear one," She grimaced at the familiarity. *There, they are gone, out of sight. And we are undetected.* "Alright, young one, but please hurry, and watch your step. One never knows what lurks in the shadows. Hurry, now."

Sarah scooched out from under the huge wing and dashed for the nearby forest. Returning shortly, she asked. "Okay, can we go home now? Grandma is probably frantic. They will probably send someone out to look for me."

"They already have, my dear, and found nothing. They have left the island."

"What? That can't be. They would never leave me behind." She frowned, jutting out her chin in disbelief.

"But child, they do not even know you are here. They have come and gone while you were yet sleeping."

"Why didn't you tell us? You are mean, and I don't like you anymore."

Like me? Why not? I'm lovable, am I not? She sniffed. "It matters not whether you like me or not. You are here for a purpose, and you will stay until that purpose is completed."

Sarah stood shaking, her hands balled into tight fists,

"You're a liar, and I hate you. You told me I could go back home whenever I wanted, and you lied. Liar, liar, pants on fire." She fumed.

"Now, now, child, hate is such a nasty word. But it doesn't matter what you think. I am in control, not you, and you will do what I say, if you ever hope to get to the outside world. Prepare to leave. We will be departing for the cavern momentarily, as soon as it is dark enough. Almost time," she cooed, a smooth edge to her dragon tongue.

Sarah stuck out her tongue, and rasp-berried her capturer.

"Oh, I'm crushed," Maggie mocked. "Regardless, of what you think of me, I have power over you, of which you shall not escape. So, it would be to your benefit to make the best of it. And Sarah, dear, never challenge me. You could regret it in ways you may not have considered. Be a good girl. Do as you are told, and you may see your family sooner than you think . . . or not." She butted Hatchet where he slept. "Get up, you lazy dolt. We have work to do."

Hatchet pushed at the huge snout. "I am no' asleepin'. I be hearin' every word you be saying. Leave me dautter alone."

"Your daughter? What do you mean by that? There's no relationship here. You must be daft." Maggie scorned.

Hatchet smiled tenderly at Sarah. "She be my dautter by adoption. She be my friend, and don't you be doin' nothin' to hurt her, or you will be accountin' to me."

Maggie laughed "And what can you do, you feeble excuse of at a man?"

"Per'aps a bit more then ye be thinkin'." He smiled, rubbing the tips of his fingers together. A small spark kindled, and he rested it on a shaft of dried grass, blowing gently as it caught fire. "I been practicin'."

"My, my, we have been learning a thing or two, haven't we? However, your magic is nothing compared to mine. But I will respect your wishes for the time being. However, we must be going. I don't want to spend another night on this frozen out-cropping. Are we ready, oh lord and master?" She bent her head in mock acquiescence. Would you prefer walking or riding? It's quite a distance, you know."

"Whatever me new dautter wishes t' do, is fin' wit' me." He turned, smiled tenderly at Sarah, and received a grateful smile in return.

Sarah studied the seemingly contrite dragon and smiled. She did so love to fly. "Well," she said, glancing at Hatchet. "If it's okay with you . . . Dad . . . I think I'd like to fly."

"Yer wish is me comman'. After you . . . dautter."

Hmm. This is a new side of Hatchet I never considered.

And this child . . . . Watch it, Maggie. Don't get sentimental.
It's a sign of weakness, remember? She extended a wing.

"Get on," she said gruffly.

"Aft'r you," Hatchet smiled and helped his new daughter to get comfortable aboard their flying steed. Settling behind her, he wrapped his arms around her waist, and said, "Let's get this overwit'." Then to Sarah. "Hang on tight, me girl. We be goin' 'ome.

Sarah shrieked with delight, spreading her arms wide, her head held back, enjoying the wind in her face. Her exuberance was contagious and soon Hatchet was laughing with her, simply for the joy of being alive, and for the little girl he had begun to love as his own.

Maggie's mind was muddled. The child was already beginning to grow on her. *Feisty, but sweet. Perhaps . . . no, she is human, and I am dragon. Enemies for centuries. I must be careful, and not succumb to the frailties of this human child. But . . . she does make life . . . interesting.* She sighed and made a beeline for home.

CHAPTER NINE

"Merlin? Can I talk to you for a minute?"

"Certainly, young knight. What's on your mind?"

"I think Sarah's on the island, but I can't be sure."

Merlin straightened just a bit, his weathered face showing marking interest. "And why would you say that, my boy?"

"I'm not sure, but I think I felt her presence as we were leaving the island."

"Really? I thought I was the only one. If she *is* there, Maggie is using powerful magic to hide her from us."

"I think we should talk to Grandpa. He knows Maggie the best. Maybe he can shine some light on what's really going on."

Merin stroked his beard. "I am hesitant to do that. It is apparent that Maggie's real desire is to get Alfred to the island, so they can be together. As we are already aware, she would do anything for the return of her master, or beloved, as she likes to say. He must not go to the island under any circumstances. The pull would be too strong, and the likelihood of bringing him back could be out of our control. Maggie is very powerful. And she is determined."

"But . . . is one dragon more powerful than five wizards, and the queen of the dragons?"

"Five?" puzzled the old wizard. "How do you come up with five?"

"Well . . . there's you and Grandpa, Dad and me . . . and . . . Grandma. She's almost a wizard. She knows magic, and she loves Grandpa, and our family, enough to protect us all."

"'tis true. A woman in love can be a formidable enemy. But this will take more power than even that."

"Not to hear Grandma tell it."

"Um, yes. And I am certain she will be a great asset, if it comes to that. But women are so emotional. And that in itself can end in disaster. I should know." He grimaced.

"I think you underestimate Grandma," Sure-shot replied, stubbornly.

"Perhaps," Merlin murmured, then nodded. "Perhaps it would be worth a try. Why don't we—"

"Why don't we what?"

Merlin swallowed and turned toward the door, a bright smile covering his elderly features. "Ah, Miss Gwenny, so lovely to hear your voice. And to what do we have the pleasure of your company?" He smiled once again, a tender, affectionate smile. "It's a delight to see you again, my dear."

Gwenny flushed and shyly returned the smile. "Um," she faltered, "it is, um, time for lunch. Er, um. Everyone is already at the table . . . except for you two. Hop to it. No one gets to eat, until all are accounted for." Her lip began to tremble. "Except for our dear Sarah, of course." Tears filled her eyes, and she dabbed at them with the hem of her apron.

Merlin rushed to her side and placed an arm around her shoulders. "Do not cry, my lady. I am certain Sarah is well."

"And how can you be so certain . . . she's gone . . . not at home where she belongs." She sniffed.

"My darling girl, Sarah is very resourceful, we all know that, and besides, Maggie needs to keep her in good order as a bargaining tool, if nothing else. If I were you, I'd be more concerned about that poor dragon . . . and Hatchet. She may talk them to death." He chuckled. "Either that, or she'll have them eating out of her hand. She's quite the charmer, you know. Just like her beloved auntie." He gently brushed away a wayward tear, before tucking a stray strand of silver hair behind one ear. He cleared his throat, as Sure-shot's jaw dropped, and his eyes widened.

"D-do you really think so?" she smiled, feeling

suddenly a bit awkward, and shy, with this stunningly handsome man, so close, so dear. She shook her head as if to clear it. "Well, um, we had best be going." She pretended to straighten her apron while gazing shyly at her guest. "Dinner is . . . getting cold, and that . . . will . . . never do."

"After you, my dear. By the way, have I mentioned how lovely you are . . . even with flour on your nose?" He grinned and tapped gently on the tip of her nose before turning to Sure-shot. "Ready, boy? We can talk during our meal. Come, come. We don't want to keep our lovely Gwenny waiting, and the rest of the family as well," he hurried to include. Clearing his throat, he offered Gwenny his arm and escorted her non-protesting body to the dining room.

Sure-shot stared after the two and gaped. *What is going on here? Anything to tell me, Merlin, you sly dog? Merlin and Aunt Gwenny? Aunt Gwenny and Merlin? Hmmmm. Nah. He's just being nice . . . I think. But what if . . . ?* He grinned and began to whistle as he followed the housekeeper and her escort on to dinner.

***

It seemed the camp was divided. Sure-shot had volunteered to go to the island, and stay with the shepherd and his family, while secretly searching for Sarah. Alfred resounded with a definite no, while the Summers family were willing to do just about anything to get Sarah back.

"We can't be certain the child is even on the island. We searched everywhere, and there was not a sign of her."

"Not everywhere, Grandpa. I know she's there. I felt her presence. Maggie has her hidden, but I know she's on that island. I know the island better than anyone . . . well, other than you and Hatchet. But I'd be the best to go. Nobody would even suspect. I'd keep a low profile, and maybe Anna, and her sisters, could help me keep an eye out. I wouldn't do anything dangerous. I'll be safe, I promise."

"I don't know, son." Robert shook his head. "Maggie is a powerful dragon with powerful senses. If she thinks you might be on the island, she may kill Sarah, and take you as hostage, knowing that your grandfather would do anything in his power to get you back."

"That's a chance I'm willing to take. Besides, Ellie can keep an eye on me. If she thinks Maggie knows I'm there, she can convince her otherwise with her dragon magic. She's a lot more powerful than Maggie is anyway. I'll be just fine, but right now I think I'm the only one who can save Sarah. Last time Maggie saw me, I was only thirteen. I'm almost fifteen, and look entirely different than I did then. Come on, Dad. I know you'll feel just awful, maybe even never forgive yourself, if something happens to Sarah. I can take care of myself. I'll be safe, I just know it."

Harriet gripped her son as tightly as she dared. "Harold, I almost lost you once. I can't take the chance of losing you again." She clung to him as if she would never let him go.

"Mom," Sure-shot whispered. "You're embarrassing me. I'll be just fine. I won't do anything foolish, and if Grandpa will send along some of that invisible stuff, whenever I go near the mountain, I'll put it on. They won't even know I'm there. Dad? Please, I have to go."

"If it will make you feel any better, Mrs. Sinclair," Brian broke in. "I'll be glad to go with him. Watch out for him, you know. Besides, four eyes are better than one any day."

"Six eyes," Belinda broke in. "If Sure-shot and Brian get to go, I should go too. She's my sister, and let's face it, the boys would be helpless without Todd and me."

"Me want to go, too." Amanda Joy toddled over to Sure-Shot and smiled into his face.

Harriet scooped up the toddler and said. "Now see what you've done. Is there no sanity in this house?"

"Harriet, dear. I think the kids have a point. Maggie is much less likely to suspect a bunch of shepherd kids, than an adult, any day. And if Todd is with them, they should be just fine."

"But Bee, don't you think that awful dragon would know a wood creature when she saw one? She could just as soon kill them all."

"I don't think so. She's not stupid. And she knows that if anything happens to these children, there will be . . . well I can't say it, but she'll know. After all, it isn't the children she wants, it's Alfred, and if any of Alfred's family or friends are harmed in any way, she will know, without a doubt, she is doomed. And besides, Todd is a shape shifter. She'll never see him coming. And I'm sure Ellie will keep an eye on the goings on, as well. I say we take a vote. Yes, or no. Should we let the children try to save Sarah."

All but two hands slowly raised, Harriet, and Alfred's, the only dissenting votes.

"Come on, people," Robert pleaded. "We need to be united on this."

"I c-can't lose my boy, I just can't." Harriet sobbed.

"Dear lady," broke in Merlin. "Would it make you feel better if I accompanied the children?"

"Merlin! You can't do that. She may think that you are Alfred, and when she finds out you are not, and she will, she may do more harm to everyone."

"Dear Mother Queen. Do you not think I have already

thought of that? But she will never know I am there. I shall disguise myself. Perhaps a bird, or a dog, or a sheep. A sheep dog. That would be perfect. Believe me, she'll never know. "

He rubbed his hands together in glee, then suddenly sobered. "My only request is that you take good care of our lovely Gwenny, and the family who stay behind." He turned to Gwenny. "I will be expecting some of your wonderful cooking when we return." He patted his stomach and licked his lips. "Do you think you could manage that? And we *will* return, I promise."

Aunt Gwenny blushed to her gray roots, at a loss for words, but slowly nodded her head. *For you, I would do practically anything.* She jumped inside. *Did I just say that? My, oh my, what has come over me.*

But Merlin just took her hand, patted it gently and smiled. "Thank you, dear lady. We will return as soon as we can." Turning to the children, he barked, "Well, what are we waiting for? Get a move on. Times a wastin'."

"Wait!" Harriet shouted. "We aren't all in one accord, yet."

"Of course, we are. I have no doubt that you, dear lady, see the wisdom in this journey, and Alfred? He is at a loss for words. But he knows in his heart this is the only solution. Isn't that right, Alfred?"

Alfred's shoulders slumped, but he nodded briefly. "Yes, it is the only way. Godspeed to all of you." He turned and hurried from the room. It would never do for anyone to see the mighty wizard, Alfred, cry. Magdalyn followed her husband as quickly as she could. Neither of them should be alone at this time of sorrow. Her family, just united, would once again be separated, but hopefully just for a time. Her own eyes dripped as she caught up with her husband and wrapped her arms around him. "It will be okay, Alfred. I can feel it in my bones, and you know my bones are always right."

But he didn't answer. There was just too much pain.

* * *

Merlin watched the couple hurry from the dining room, pain reflected in his own eyes. But what must be done, must be done. A sense of urgency filled his soul. He turned toward the children "Well, um, I think it's time we be on our way."

"But we're not ready yet," Belinda protested.

Merlin raised his right hand in a circular manner. "We're not?" he asked, as he disappeared, and a shaggy mongrel stood in his place.

Belinda gasped as she fingered her shepherdess robes and then began to giggle at Sure-shot and Brian. "You guys look so cute. So . . . shepherdy. And Merlin, you look great as a dog, even with your beard."

"What?" With a clumsy paw, Merlin swiped at the long white chin hairs, barking once, as the beard disappeared. "There, is that any better?" he asked, his happy tail twitching in delight.

"Much," giggled Belinda. "You make an adorable puppy." She cooed.

"Puppy?" he groused. "I'll have you know I am Merlin, the wonder pooch."

"Okay, okay," Belinda giggled. "Well, I guess we *are* ready to go. Oh, wait. We can't forget Todd."

"Do not worry, Belinda Girl. Todd is here, ready to go, yes he is."

Belinda grimed and said, "Okay, we're all here. Let's do it to it."

"As you wish, young mistress," Merlin woofed, and the six would-be rescuers disappeared.

"Harold," Harriet cried as she reached toward the now empty space, where Merlin and the children had once stood. "He never even said good-bye," she whimpered, as she collapsed into her husband's arms.

CHAPTER TEN

"I'll get it!" Anna shouted as she ran toward the only door.

"Be careful, Anna. You know not what lies beyond. It could be—" But Anna paid no attention to her father as she threw open the door and began to shriek. "Da, it's Sure-shot, and Brian, and Belinda, and . . . and a dog. A real dog, for herding . . . sheep. Can we keep them, Da?"

"Who?" grinned Da. "The people or the dog? Welcome," he bellowed, as he drew Belinda into his friendly arms, and nodded at the boys in delight. "What have you got here?" he asked as he reached down to pet the scruffy dog.

"Touch me not," growled the dog. "I am Merlin, the great wizard, and am not used to being touched by a mere peasant. If we may be admitted to your abode, I shall show my true self, and let you know the nature of our business."

The shepherd gaped at the talking dog and quickly ushered the group into his humble home.

"Ah, much better." Merlin, now as a man, shook out his robes, straightened his pointed hat and grinned at the astounded shepherd.

"Pretty cool, wouldn't you say?" Merlin stood and waited for an answer from his stunned host.

The shepherd peered out the door. "Seems a mite warm t' me," he said, a bit confused.

"No, no, Da," Anna giggled. "Sure-shot taught me that in the outside world, cool means good . . . kinda." She gazed at the boy, in such a way, he blushed from head to toe. "Didn't you, Sure-shot. I'm so glad you came back. Can you stay . . . maybe . . . forever?" She grinned, obvious adoration sparkling in her eyes.

"Child, child," boomed Merlin. "Perhaps not forever, but we would be grateful if you could provide shelter for a few days. You see, the black dragon has taken our Sarah, and we must get her back. We need your help to hide us from the wicked one, whilst we search. We need a cover . . . so to speak."

"A cover?" repeated the confused shepherd.

"He means, sir," Sure-shot broke in, "that we need a place to stay where the dragon can't find us, 'cause if she doesn't know we're on the island, she won't know we're here to rescue Sarah."

"Oh, Da. Sarah's been captured. We have to do something. We can't let them hurt Sarah. She's my friend, even if she does want Sure-shot for her own." She frowned. "We have to save her, Da. We just have to."

"We'll do our best, my child. In the mean, please come in and make yourself comfortable. Anna, will you see to our guests needs?"

"Right away, Da." She smiled at Sure-shot before running off to put the kettle on for tea.

Sure-shot stared at the young woman running off to care for the needs of her guests, and asked. *Who is that? It can't be Anna, even though it does look something like her. But this girl is older, and . . . and . . . beautiful.* Quickly changing the subject, he asked, "Where is Evangeline? Doesn't she usually fix the tea?"

The shepherd chuckled. "My boy, you are too late. You were gone s' long, she was forced to wed another . . . but alas," he sighed, "not one to work the sheep. He's a village boy. But she seems happy, and she is now with child. Our first grand."

"Married . . . pregnant . . . . But she's too young."

"Sixteen, she was, when she tied the knot. She's most seventeen as we speak. May be she'll drop by, while yer here. I'm sure she'd love t' see ye. Ye haven't much changed, though, have ye boy. Seems ye'd do more growin' in three years."

"Three years? Has it been that long? So that would make Anna—"

"Almost fourteen years, now. Just right for marriage, wouldn't ye say, boy?"

Anna kept her back to her guests, her face burning, and not from the stove, mentally chiding her father, for saying anything at all. Though marriage to Sure-shot was still constantly on her mind, she knew that was just a childish wish, and Sure-shot had made it plain, he was far too young for such thoughts. *But*, she sighed, *it would have been nice.*

* * *

Sarah grimaced, dipping one more plate in the soapy water. This was not what she had in mind. *I'm here to help Hatchet, not bury myself in dish water.* She frowned, and stuck out her tongue at the piles of dirty dishes. *Who eats this much anyway? It doesn't look like anyone's touched this kitchen in years.* She sighed and rinsed a cup. *You're lucky I don't throw you at the nasty, lying, Maggie, but she'd probably burn you to a puddle of molten pewter, and then what would we use to drink from.* She scowled.

"Dautter, do you be needin' some assistance? I am very gud at dryin'."

Sarah stared at Hatchet for just a moment and grinned. There he stood with an oversized apron covering his middle, and a crooked chef's hat on his head, with a drying towel draped haphazardly over his arm.

"Well, dautter, kin I be of service t' ye? It's no bein' loikely ye'll get any 'elp from the black demon."

"Who, Maggie? No, I don't suppose so. She's a liar and a bully. Why do you put up with her?"

"Well, me dautter. She may be a mean, nasty, bully, as ye say, but she's gonna 'elp me get me fut back. She promised."

"And you believe her? I think she's just using you to get what she wants. Then when she's through with you, she'll throw you away like dirty dishwater."

"Per'aps. But in the mean, I 'ave me wunnerful dautter frien'. And besides, Maggie's not s' bad, once ye git to know 'er. In fact, she's not so bad as ye might think."

"No, she's worse."

"Now, dautter. Why not give 'er a chance? She moight jest grow on ye . . . aft'r a bit. Ye moight just learn t' loike her."

"Humph. I don't think so, but I'll try, if you think it might do any good. But only for you."

Hatchet smiled at the little girl. *She is growing up so fast.* Hardly a little girl anymore, but she was still his dautter, after a fashion, and he loved her. *Besides, if bein' nice t' Maggie will 'elp keep 'er safe, so be it.*

* * *

Maggie stood in the hall, just outside the kitchen doorway, and listened to this strange conversation, her massive head cocked to one side, her eyes puzzled. Hatchet was sticking up for her? *My, my, what a change.* She smiled softly. *What do you know? There may be hope for him yet.* An unfamiliar stirring in her chest made her jump inside. *Now, now, Maggie, let's not get sentimental.* She turned and quietly strolled down the hall to the nursery. *Oh, Hatchet, what are you doing to me?*

CHAPTER ELEVEN

Sarah sighed and smiled at the outlaw. "You're doing super, Hatchet, er, I mean . . . um, Dad." She giggled, as Hatchet blushed, fumbling with the chalk at the makeshift slate board.

"You—make it—easy—to learn, dautter." Hatchet took great care in pronouncing each word, exactly as he had been taught.

"Maggie will be so proud of you. And me, too," she hastened to add.

"Yer proud of me?" he asked.

"The proudest. You, um, Dad, are a quick learner, and smart, too. Even Alfred would be proud of you."

Hatchet sat up a little straighter. It didn't matter what Alfred, or Maggie, for that matter, thought. As long as his dautter was proud of him, he was okay. "You—think—I'm smart?" He grinned at the little girl.

"Oh, absolutely . . . the smartest. Look how much you've already learned. It took me years to learn all this stuff."

"It did? It seems—easy enough." The sentences were coming easier, now, with Sarah's help. "You make a good teacher, dautter. Much better than Maggie. She can get a little . . . well, you know."

"Well, Maggie isn't exactly a model of charm, and sweetness." She frowned. "Maybe if I got to know her a little better, we could be friends . . . or at least not so much enemies. But she had better start learning to tell the truth, and not lie so much."

"Dautter, be very kearful where Maggie be concerned. She be a bit hot headed, and not so trustworthy, if ye be knowin' w'at I mean."

"Then why are you staying with her?"

"Weel, 'oi, um, *I* tol' you a'ready. She said she would be tryin' to fix me fut, so I need to 'elp 'er fer jest a bit more."

"Hatchet . . . er, Dad, you're slipping back into your old way of speaking. I think she will respect you more if she knows how hard you are trying to learn to speak proper like. And you're doing a fantastic job, even if I do say so, myself." Sarah grinned at the pleased expression on Hatchet's face. "Besides, I think she likes you in spite of what she says . . . I know I do." She flushed and turned back to the slate board.

"You do? I like you, too. You are like the dautter I never had. You won't ever leave me, will you?"

"Well . . . um, Dad . . . I *will* have to go back to where I belong, someday, but I'll stay and help you as long as I can." She brightened. "And I can always come back and visit, if you'd like."

"O'i would loike tha' vera much. O'i won't be so lonesome, knowin' ye will be comin' back t' visit."

"'*I*' . . . um, Dad. Remember? '*I*', not o'i, but '*I*.' Maggie will really like it if you can remember. You do like Maggie, don't you? I can tell. She may be a big ol' meanie sometimes, but I think she has a good heart in there somewhere. Don't you think?"

"Weel, I might uv seen a bit of gud in her on occasion. And she is vera beautiful, do ye not think?" He flushed once again, as Sarah grinned.

"I knew you liked her. So, do I . . . sometimes. But I don't know if she wants us to like her. I think she wants to be tough, and not vulnerable. To be in control of everything, because of who she is. But I like her anyway. I love Ellie, and Blue, but Maggie is beginning to grow on me, just a bit. She does have her moments." Sarah sighed.

Maggie, invisible to the two, listened intently, until she could listen no more. Silently, she shifted just a bit, before spreading her massive wings and taking to the skies. She had much to think about.

* * *

Mr. Merlin," Anna interrupted. "I'm sorry, but do you really think Sarah might be here on the island?"

"Unfortunately, I do. But Maggie undoubtedly has her hidden where we shall not soon find her . . . without a little luck, I'd say, on our side."

"But why do you think she might be here? Didn't you already check the island?"

"We did, but when Sure-shot suggested we try again, I—"

"Sure-shot?" She glanced at the boy sitting at the end of the table. "Why would Sure-shot—"

"Sure-shot and Sarah have a special connection. He just feels that she is here, and so do I. We just have to find out where she is, and take her home before something bad happens to her. Do you understand, my dear girl?"

Anna did understand . . . all too well, but it hurt knowing the boy she was so taken with, might have feelings for another. But she nodded, and said, "Yes, sir. I understand completely, and I will do my best to try and find her. Sarah and I have a lot in common, and I don't want to see her get hurt." *Even if I lose Sure-shot in the process.* Her eyes filled with tears, and to those watching, she seemed emotionally overwrought by the loss of her friend, and they seemed sympathetic, which wasn't at all helpful, or maybe it was, in a different way.

She cried inside, but no one must ever know her feelings of loss. *Sure-shot and Sarah.* She loved them both. But how could she choose between them. She couldn't, so she wouldn't even try. She returned to the soup pot and began to fill the large wooden bowls with the savory stew, hoping her tears wouldn't add unnecessary salt to her offering.

Sure-shot watched Anna with concern, wishing he could help, but knowing he could not. Right now, his primary concern was to rescue Sarah. After that? Who knew?

Belinda watched Sure-shot. A tinge of something came over her at his obvious attention to Anna. Jealousy, perhaps? *Nah, Anna's just a kid.* She startled. *But not so much anymore.* Her heart hurt, just a little, and a tear filled her eye as she realized she no longer appeared to be first in Sure-shot's affection. She sighed. Those around her were certain her thoughts were of her lost sister, and she would never let them know otherwise.

She squeezed Brian's hand, just a little, but his mind, as

well, seemed to be occupied elsewhere. She folded her hands in her lap and cried inside. She no longer seemed to be important to anyone. But this was not about Belinda, it was about Sarah, and her swift return. She smiled bravely through her tears.

Merlin watched Belinda out of the corner of his eye, concerned for this brave young warrior but knowing all would be right in the end. It had to be. It just had to be.

* * *

It was getting late, and Sarah's stomach began to growl. Um . . . uh . . . Hatch—I mean, Dad? I think we've worked hard enough for now. It's getting close to dinner time, and I think we better get something to eat. We can start again tomorrow."

"You have spoken well, dautter. We must be getting' about supper. If you will be checkin' the larder, Oi'll, I mean *I* will chop the fir'wood and set the stove to the ready."

Sarah grinned as she accepted the outlaw's hand and jumped to her feet. "Let's go eat."

CHAPTER TWELVE

Something was strange . . . not wrong exactly, but strange. The firewood lay in neat stacks and the air smelled wonderful.

Hatchet stared at Sarah for just a moment, and grinned. "The marster must be back. Per'aps he be making supper. Come, dautter. We mustn't ke'p the marster waitin'."

But stranger still, when they opened the kitchen door, Alfred was not present. Instead, a tall woman, dressed entirely in black - her long black hair, with purple streaks - stood at the stove, stirring something they hoped tasted as good as it smelled.

"Well, don't just stand there, looking like starving children. Come in and shut the door. Sit down and get ready to eat. My treat, of course."

Hatchet stared at Sarah, and Sarah stared back at Hatchet. *Who? What?*

"Don't make me ask you twice. I've worked hard on this meal, and I'd like to be shown a little appreciation."

"M-Maggie?" Sarah stuttered. "Is that . . . you?"

"And who else would it be, child?" She turned and stared pointedly at Sarah.

Sarah blinked and cautiously strolled toward the woman at the stove. As if in a trance, Hatchet hobbled to the heavy metal table and sat down. This beautiful woman could not possibly be the black devil/dragon, Maggie. It sounded like her, but . . . it couldn't be. He plopped into the chair at the end of the table and watched, mesmerized, as Sarah began speaking to this stranger.

"I-I don't know, but you don't look like our Maggie."

"And why not, child?" The woman asked.

"Y-you're a woman, but you can't be, 'cause Maggie is a dragon, and you're not. What did you do with Maggie?" she demanded, her hands on her hips, her eyes flashing.

"But, child, it truly is me. Look in my eyes. Can't you see me?"

"But . . . how . . . why . . . Are you trying to trick us? It's not nice to try to trick people." She glared at the woman.

"Child, it is not polite to stare. I thought I would surprise you, as you two have been working so hard, and fix you dinner. But I could hardly do that as a dragon, could I?"

"I-I guess not, but—"

"But what, child? Am I that ugly you cannot speak?"

"Oh, no. It's just that you don't look anything like our Maggie." She stared at the ebony woman. "And your skin is . . . black."

"Does that distress you, child, that I am black. Here, see if this is any better." With a wave of her hand, her skin faded to a creamy brown, then a satiny white. "Now do you feel more comfortable?"

"Not really. You are very beautiful as any color, but I like you best as . . . black. Change back, please."

Maggie was prepared to be offended at the child, but instead, was pleasantly surprised at this sweet child's words. "As you wish," she flushed, waving her hand and once again became the black beauty, Maggie, the woman.

"How did you do that?" breathed Sarah.

"I am dragon, after all. And dragons are magical creatures. However, we black dragons are not naturally shape shifters, but it is possible when necessary. And I found it necessary to prepare the meal. Is that all right with you, child?"

"Oh, absolutely. What are you cooking? It smells wonderful, doesn't it Hatchet, er, Dad?" She smiled first at Maggie and then at Hatchet. But Hatchet was at a loss for words, so he nodded, and smiled as a pink flush covered his neck and ears.

"Can I help you, Maggie," Sarah asked, "with anything?"

"Not at this time, child. Just enjoy. Now, please be seated. Dinner is about to be served."

Sarah hurried to the table as platters of roasted potatoes and rich meats, floated to the table and settled there. Maggie took her place at the opposite end of the table and allowed Sarah the privilege of reciting the mealtime prayer.

After dinner, Hatchet insisted on cleaning up. His mind *Maggie . . . Sarah . . . Maggie . . . .*

"Come, child, I would talk with thee a bit . . . if you don't mind." Maggie turned toward the door leading to the cavern hallway.

"Haven't we been talking?"

"Well, yes. But I have something special I would like to discuss, if you can keep a secret, that is."

"A secret? I love secrets." Sarah bubbled. "But what about Hatchet . . . I mean . . . Dad? Can he know the secret, too?"

"All in good time, child. Now is the time I must reveal to you alone. Do you understand?"

"Not exactly, but I'm game if you are."

"Game? What does that mean . . . game? Isn't that something you eat?"

"Sometimes. But this kind of game means I'm willing to talk if you are. But does um . . . Dad know what we're going to talk about, or can we tell him later?"

"He does not. Perhaps, and perhaps not. We shall see."

"See what?"

"Child, you are trying my patience. Do you, or do you not, want to hear what I have to tell you?"

"Oh, yes. I love stories/"

"This is not merely a story, but my history," she miffed. "But you must speak of this to no one, until I decide what I am about to reveal to you will be accepted properly. Now come. You like to fly, don't you? So, climb aboard. We will talk when we get there."

"When we get where? Why can't you tell me now?"

Maggie sighed. "Child! Just climb aboard, and I will tell you when the time is right."

* * *

Sure-shot gazed at the night sky, and suddenly froze. A high-pitched squeal, and what sounded like a deep chuckle filled the air for just a moment, and he was certain the sound came from Sarah, but he could see nothing to substantiate it. "Sarah?" he shouted to the Heavens but heard nothing in return. "Probably just wishful thinking," he muttered.

"About what?" a voice to his left whispered, scanning

the sky for himself.

"Huh?" Sure-shot turned toward the voice. "Óh, hi, Merlin. What are you doing out here?"

"I was about to ask you the same thing. It's getting dark, and a bit cool, wouldn't you say? We need to get our rest. Tomorrow is going to be a busy day. Gotta find our girl, you know. And what is this 'wishful thinking' all about?"

"Ah, probably nothing, but I came out for just a bit of fresh air, and thinking time, and I thought I heard a sound that sounded a lot like Sarah, and something like a low rumble as well. I think my overactive imagination is working overtime."

"Most likely, my boy, most likely. However, nothing seems to be needing attending at this hour, so let's go back inside and get some rest. Okay, son?"

"Whatever you say, sir. But it really did sound like—"

"Um . . yes, but it is far too late to see anything at this hour. We will start again at dawn. Now, in with you, young man."

Merlin searched the dusky sky, for just a moment, as he ushered Sure-shot back into the warmth of the shepherd's cozy cabin. *Difficult to see much when it's dusky. Time enough on the morrow to attend to such things.* But still he worried.

CHAPTER THIRTEEN

Well, child, did you like our little jaunt? Was it to your satisfaction?" Maggie smiled softly at the child before settling more comfortably on the rocky ledge and wrapping one wing around the shivering little girl.

"It was fantastical," Sarah gushed. "But I thought I heard Sure-shot calling my name. That's not possible, is it?"

"Not likely, my dear. But let's talk of pleasanter things, shall we?"

"Okay, but can we talk about it later?"

"Perhaps. We shall see, but first I need to tell you my story, and also to ask your opinion on something." Sarah's opinion was the least of her concerns, but if she could win the child's confidence, perhaps she could learn a better way for the return of her beloved Alfred. "Now, where shall we start? I know. Why do you think those people are trying to keep my beloved away from me?"

Sarah was surprised. This was hardly what she expected to hear. "I thought we were going to talk about your secret, the reason we're here, not about Alfred."

"We will, child. But first—"

"I would really appreciate it if you would quit calling me child. I am not a child. I am big, and my name is Sarah."

"Ah, so you are, and so it is. All right, child, I mean, Sarah. I will do my best if you will do yours and try to understand where I am coming from. Alfred is my life, and I cannot understand why he was taken from me, and why he appears to want to stay with . . . with that woman, he calls wife. Alfred belongs to me. He saved my life, and I am indebted to him, and have learned to love him deeply. What can she give him that I cannot?"

"Well, Maggie, first of all, Alfred is human, and Magdalyn is human, and she is his wife, the love of his life."

"That's a lie!" Maggie bristled. "I am the love of his life. He told me so."

"But, Maggie," Sarah sympathized. "That was when he thought Magdalyn was dead and that he would never see her again. I'm sure Alfred cares for you a whole lot, but his first loyalty is to his first love. Do you understand?"

Maggie removed her wing from around Sarah and sniffed. "You lie, and I told you we cannot speak if you lie to me. Perhaps I will leave you on this ledge, until you think about telling me what I want to hear. We're a long way from home," she smirked.

Sarah shivered. "And what good would that do? You would be all alone, with no one to care for you, or pay any attention to you . . . ever."

"Again, you lie. I have Hatchet, and simple as he is, he would never abandon me."

"Are you c-certain?" Sarah quivered. "Y-you haven't been very nice to him, and *I* am his, um, daughter. W-who do you think he would choose, if he had to? Someone who treats him badly or the daughter he loves? If we work together, maybe we will all get what we want, even if it's not what we think it is. Well?"

"Hmmm, perhaps you are right, and perhaps not, but I see the reasoning behind your statement, so I will try . . . for a time at least." Maggie slowly slipped her wing back around the little girl and sighed. "Did you know that I am a princess?"

"Really? Sarah beamed, warming just a bit. "Did you know that Sarah means 'princess?' Maybe we have more in common than we thought. We're both royalty . . . after a fashion. Now, tell me about your secret. I am so excited to hear about it. Does anyone else know? Are you going to be a queen someday, and rule your own country? That would be so cool. I will never be a queen, but you would make a great one."

"Tell that to my father," Maggie miffed. "He chose my sister over me, his first born, to rule Dragon Island. It's not right, it just isn't right. And my mother sided with him. I can't believe it, her own daughter."

"But aren't you and Ellie sisters?"

"Half-sisters. My real mother died of the sickness, soon after my egg was laid." She stared into space. "Ellie's mother was second wife, and she raised me as her own. When I was just a few years of age, the sickness returned, and I was very ill. Alfred saved my life, and brought me here to wizard island, to keep me safe, you see. Many eggs were sent with us, for their safely and protection, and so that no more dragon lives would be lost. Even though I was very young, I cared for those eggs until they hatched. Ellie was one of the hatchlings. I loved her as one of my own, and this is how she repaid me, by stealing my rightful place as queen.

"We lost a lot of dragons, due to the sickness. But Alfred was able to combat it, and most of us are now surviving, fortunately for mankind, as well as dragonkind. Do you understand, I almost died, but then Alfred found me and healed me, and that is why I am devoted to him . . . forever."

"But loving someone, because they saved your life, is not the same thing as loving someone as a lifelong companion."

"But he loved me. I know he did, and he will love me again, I just know it."

"And I think you are right. You will always be special to him, but Magdalyn is the love of his life . . . his first true love."

Maggie thought about this for just a moment, and abruptly changed the topic. "My ancestor was a great warrior . . . a ruler of his people. He too loved a human, but she also married another. I suppose that is something we have in common . . . my great-great-great-grandfather and me. I would love to have met him." She smiled wistfully. "Perhaps he could have taught me a thing, or too, about humans. He was the greatest warrior of all time. Like me, he was as black as night, and as brave as . . . well, he was the bravest. Even though it got him into trouble, occasionally, I understand. His name was Chi."

"Chi? Lark's Chi?"

"Why, yes, Sarah. How did you know about my ancestor?

"Merlin told us. He is a descendant of Lark, the great Wizard, and—"

"That, that imposter is a descendant of our great mother, Lark?"

"Yes, and he's the one who painted the pictures, and

brought them to life so that Alfred could be born and save your life. You'd like him, if you got to know him."

"Perhaps. We shall see."

"Who was Ellie's ancestor. Do you know?"

"Unfortunately, yes. Perhaps that is the reason she was chosen to be . . . queen . . . over me, who should have rightly been."

"Well, what was her name?"

"Her name was Atara, the first queen of the dragons. She should have mated with Chi, but she saw him more of a younger brother, than a mate, I have been told. My, just think of where we would be with Atara and Chi as our dragon parents." She sighed. "But alas, it was not to be. Black must mate with black and silver with silver, I suppose."

"And human with human." Sarah spoke softly.

"What? But Alfred is both human and dragon. He is magic, powerful."

"Yes, but his dragon-hood is because of magic, not because he was born dragon."

"But . . . we could have been happy as dragon, couldn't we? He could have changed to dragon, forever, had it not been for that, that other person."

"Would you have been willing to change into a human

for all eternity, for him?"

"Unfortunately, that would not be an option. He would have to become dragon. I would most likely lose all my dragon abilities, if I were simply human. No, no, it would . . . never . . . do. Hmmm. But it is a thought. Do you think he would love me still, if I gave up my dragon life for him? Certainly, that other person could not compete."

"Under different circumstances, maybe, but you have to remember, Alfred met and married Magdalyn long before he met you. And he is just a painting, in a painted world. I'm sure he would still like to be friends, though, if you were, um, willing."

Maggie thought for a moment and said, "Never. I am afraid it is much too late for that. It would be far too painful watching him with that other woman. No, he will have to make a choice– the love of a mere woman, or the love of one who truly has his best interests at heart – his magical interest as well. Can she, a mere mortal, assist him with his most wonderful magic? I don't think so." She smiled a confident dragon smile.

"Well, Maggie, I hate to tell you this, and don't get mad, but Magdalyn does have magical abilities. And she is also of the painted world, and she loves her husband enough to fight for him, if necessary."

"A mere mortal fight me, the progeny of the greatest warrior that has ever been?"

"You know what they say about the love of a good woman, and the power it holds."

"Still, there is nothing like the love of a dragon to surpass any human love."

"Maybe, and maybe not, but if I were you, I wouldn't take any chances. I've seen what she can do, and with the two of them together, I'm afraid—"

"No one is more powerful than I."

"Maybe, and maybe not, but why take the chance? Why don't you find someone more suited to you and your wishes?

"Hey, I have an idea. Why don't you get to know Hatchet, um, Dad, a little better? I know he likes you. I think he thinks you're beautiful."

"Who? The idiot, the simple-minded dolt? I'm surprised at you. An intelligent young girl like you, thinking that . . . hmmm. No, it would never work. Alfred is my love and will always be. Let's not talk about it anymore."

"Well, okay, if you think so, but I still think—"

"Quiet, child. You know nothing. We will discuss this no longer. We must leave. It is getting quite chilly. Climb aboard. We shall not speak of this again." *At least for tonight,* she murmured.

"By the way, Maggie," Sarah added, comfortably astride the huge dragon, "if you ever talk about Dad in that way again, you will have me to deal with. And that won't be a pretty picture. Dad *is* smart, *and* loving, and *HE* saved *MY* life, so don't you dare ever call him an idiot or stupid again, you hear?"

My, my, wherein does such loyalty lie? Perhaps I have been a bit premature in my thinking. I will reflect on that. "As you wish, child . . . Princess Sarah." *For now.* And they flew toward the dragon's lair.

CHAPTER FOURTEEN

Gwenny paced the great room, occasionally stopping by the castle painting to stare into its recesses.

"Gwenny, dear, go to bed. Pacing and watching are not going to bring them back any sooner. They're in good hands. They have Merlin, and they have Todd. What could go wrong? They will be fine, and they *will* bring Sarah home with them, I'm certain."

"I hear what you're saying, but I notice you're still here – and Robert, and Paul, and Alfred, and Magdalyn, and—"

The queen mother sighed. "If you won't go to bed, at least sit down for a bit. You're wearing out the carpet. The children will be fine. They've been through many an adventure and have come out okay, haven't they?"

"Yes, and I trust Todd . . . and Merlin, to keep them safe. But he is old, and that . . . that outlaw is in cahoots with that horrible black dragon, and who knows what will happen to him . . . I mean them. I am so worried."

"About the kids, or Merlin? He will be okay. He is a descendant of the greatest wizard that ever was, and he knows more about magic, and these paintings than anyone could ever know. A single black dragon is no match for Merlin the Great."

"So, you say. But that menace is not alone. That horrible man, Hatchet, is with her, and no telling what mischief the two of them together might make. What if someone gets hurt?"

"If I may interject." Alfred stepped up to the painting and stared thoughtfully at it. "Hatchet shouldn't be a problem, although he could possibly be of *some* use to Maggie. But it's doubtful. Hatchet is not the brightest gem in the treasure chest, and I have seen some signs of goodness in him. And besides, he really likes the child. And he thinks she cares for him, as well. I think Sarah may have an ally in Hatchet."

"But is that affection strong enough to circumvent the evil intentions of that dragon. If she harms one hair on his, um, anyone's head, I will personally track her down, and—" She pounded her fist in her hand.

"Gwenny, calm down." Bee threw an arm around her best friend and whispered. "He will be all right, and so will the children. We just have to trust in his judgement. They will all be home soon enough, so why don't you start working on their welcome home dinner? You know how

Merlin loves your home cooked chicken and dumplings."

"He does, doesn't he. Do you think he, um, *they* would like chicken and dumplings for their welcome home meal, or do you think they would like something different? Nothing is too good for our adventurers, don't you think?"

"I, for one," Paul drooled. "love your C and D. In fact, I could eat your chicken and dumplings every day of the week. Yipes, I'm getting hungry again."

"When are you not hungry?" giggled Gretchen. "But I agree with Bee and Paul. Chicken and dumplings sound delicious. Do you need any help?"

"Well, I guess that settles that. Chicken and dumplings, it is." She turned toward the great room door and straightened her dress. "I'll be in the kitchen . . . if anyone needs me. But, if you hear anything, or see anything, you come get me immediately. And Gretchen, if you really mean it, I could use some company." *He better not bring home any fleas,* she grunted to herself.

"It would be my pleasure." Gretchen followed Gwenny to the door, and both women quickly hurried to the kitchen to begin a welcome feast. For certainly, a feast would be warranted, wouldn't it?

Bee watched her best friend hurry from the great room with worried tears in her eyes. *Oh, Gwenny. I had no idea he meant so much to you. He will return, I'm certain of it. In the meantime we must wait and pray.*

* * *

"Rise and shine, young knights, and ladies, of course. It is time to rescue the young princess."

"First, a good breakfast is in order."

Merlin sniffed the air. "My word, child, have you been up all night. What a sumptuous sight. And it smells wonderful, too. Almost as good as our own Gwenny's. No offense. She is a superb cook as well." He rubbed his stomach. Thoughts of Gwenny occupied his mind, and a marked loneliness filled his being. *She is a fine woman, our Gwenny. Let's get this over with and return home.* But aloud, he said. "You will make a fine wife, someday. Yum. Let's eat."

"I am not a child, Mr. Merlin. And I am of marriageable age *now* . . . if anyone is . . . interested." She blushed.

"But until that time comes, let us eat, and think about this captivating matter at another time." Merlin strode quickly to the rough wooden table and sat down. "Come, come, everyone. Our young hostess has prepared a lovely meal, and we must make good use of it." He licked his lips, and picked up a fork. "Well . . . anybody hungry besides me?"

He grinned as a mass of starving bodies plopped into the remaining chairs. He held up his hands for silence. "Great Creator," he prayed. "Bless this food . . . quickly, so we can eat. Amen."

* * *

Sarah rose, yawned, sniffed the air, and shuffled to the kitchen. *It smells wonderful in here.* The old wood stove glowed from freshly lit kindling, and a cozy warmth spread throughout the room. But no one was in sight. "Hello? Is anyone here?" But she received no answer.

A fresh slab of sliced bacon sizzled in the cast iron frying pan, while a large bowl of eggs waited to be scrambled, set carefully on the counter nearby. Strong black coffee bubbled in the pot on the back burner, and Sarah hurried to turn if off before it evaporated into nothingness. Coffee wasn't her favorite beverage, but when it was all that was available, you learned to make do.

Determined to make herself useful, she hurried to the cupboard, seized three pewter plates, with cups, and then grabbed the knives and forks necessary for their meal. Within minutes the table was set and waiting for Maggie and Hatchet to appear. The strong smell of bacon wafted toward her and she ran to the stove to turn it down before it began to burn. She knew what to do. After all, she had watched Gwenny cook a number of times and felt at ease in the kitchen.

While the bacon sizzled, she grabbed another skillet, placed a bit of butter, or at least she hoped it was butter, into the hot pan, and quickly stirred in the eggs. While the eggs cooked, she quickly rinsed and dried the bowl the eggs had been in, preparing it to receive the scrambled eggs . . . as soon as they were done.

She smiled to herself as she continuously stirred the eggs, occasionally turning the bacon, as needed. She didn't dare let them burn. Food was precious on the island. She didn't know where Hatchet . . . or Maggie . . . got the food, but it shouldn't be wasted.

She felt all grown up as she continued to cook the bacon and stir the eggs. *Where is everybody?* she pondered, glancing about the room. Something mighty important must have come up for them to leave the kitchen in such a hurry. *I'm going to have to scold them for leaving the bacon unwatched.*

But her primary concern was not that of burning bacon, but rather where everyone had disappeared to and for what reason. Her stomach began to flutter, and she began to worry.

"Oops. The bacon is done, and so are the eggs. What do

I do first?" Grabbing a potholder, she removed the bacon from the burner, grabbed the pan with the eggs and scraped them into the waiting bowl. Spreading a small drying towel smoothly on the counter, she gripped the bacon tongs firmly, and quickly placed each slice of bacon, on the material to drain. Aunt Gwenny used a newspaper covered with a paper towel to drain the bacon, but Sarah didn't have the luxury of doing that, so she used what was available.

"You are doing a mighty fine job, young miss. As good as I've seen for some time now."

Sarah jerked her head around and scanned the kitchen but saw no one. "Who's there?" she demanded, grabbing the spatula. "I'm well-armed. Show yourself." She swung the spatula as she began scrutinizing the kitchen.

"Relax, young one. It is just me, or I, whatever good grammar dictates. Up here . . . on the second shelf, left side. Rocky's the name, and I like you. You're a good girl. I can tell."

Sarah's gaze slowly swept the pantry and soon came face to face with the little golem. "Rocky? Sure-shot's Rocky?"

"Well, after a fashion. Technically Max is the boy's golem. I am his brother. But I know Sure-shot and Robert quite well. I was their communicator on this side of the worlds. Very nice people, but Robert was a bit strange at first. However, we got along famously after we got to know one another a little better. How are they doing? I miss them. I wish they would come back for a visit, now and then." The golem sighed, a tear glistening on his cheek."

"If you really are a golem, you better not cry. Water can dissolve you; you know."

"It can? Oh, dear. I had best watch that, had I not? No need for an early demise, is there."

Sarah couldn't help but smile at the golem and reached out a hand to touch him.

"Careful!" he shrieked. "You have that *weapon* with you. I do not want to be scraped off my shelf with a spatula." He grinned at the little girl waving the utensil.

"Oh, sorry about that. I wouldn't really try to hurt you. You just startled me, is all."

"I knew it. I was just funning with you. By the way, nobody is supposed to know about me, so hush, hush is the word. You can't tell anyone I am here. I am the eyes and ears for the young master and the wizard's son, Robert. You must keep my secret, or all could be lost."

"Sarah studied the golem for just a moment. "O-kay, I'll keep your secret, for now. I like you. You're funny. Hey, do you know where everyone went?

"Dautter, where ye be?"

"In here, um, Dad. Working on breakfast. You're just on time."

"That is not your father," whispered Rocky. "That is an evil man set to hurt my master and his family. Beware, child."

"Who . . . Hatchet?" she whispered back. "He's okay. He's my friend, and he just likes to call me his daughter . . . to protect me."

"Protect you? I think not. He is in league with the wicked black dragon. Beware, child. Beware."

As Hatchet lumbered into the kitchen, Rocky once more became stiff and hardened, now, to the average eye, nothing more than a stone toy.

"Mmmm. Smells mighty gud in here." He glanced about the room. "But where is the black menace, er, Maggie?" He smiled affectionately, but guardedly. "Somethin' mighty important must uv come up to leave afore breakfast. Did she say where she was off to?"

"Nope. I smelled bacon cooking, so I woke up and came in here, but nobody was around, so I finished up the bacon and eggs, myself. And I set the table, and everything." She grinned proudly.

"Ye did all this? Yer a girl of many talents, dautter. But

it don't seem right, Maggie leaving food cooking and not bein' here to watch it. Strange, that is. Well, with 'er, or without 'er, we can't let all this gud food go t' waste. Let's eat."

"But shouldn't we wait just a few more minutes? I'm sure she didn't mean to be gone so long."

"Well, five minutes, then. Food's getting' cold. Don't want that, now, do we." He licked his lips and drooled with anticipation. Ten minutes later, *father* and *daughter*, sat down to a cooling breakfast without the beautiful Maggie, as she had not yet returned, and stomachs were beginning to growl. *Yum.* Rocky stood at his post and watched the happy duo, his mind racing, contemplating this strange occurrence.

CHAPTER FIFTEEN

Merlin bounded through the tall grasses, occasionally stopping to roll on the ground with jubilation. *Being a dog isn't so bad*, but then he thought of Gwenny. *But being human is better.* He smiled to himself, but then quickly sobered. No time for thoughts of romance at the present. *After we rescue our small princess there will be time enough to think of such things.*

He crouched low in the grasses and waited for his first playful victim to pass.

"Has anyone seen Merlin?" Brian shouted to his comrades. "I know he's around here, somewhere. . . . Gotcha!" Brian grinned as the startled wizard jumped at this strange turn-about in who was stalking whom.

"Young man. Do you realize how old I am, and what your attack might do to me?"

"Hey, I was only playing *your* game. I just got you first."

"T'aint fair," the wizard grunted good-naturedly. "I am the wizard. You are but a mere boy. I must be losing my senses . . . for you to find me like that. However, I will forgive you if you scratch me behind my left ear."

As Brian reached out to scratch the dog behind his ear, Merlin's rough, doggie tongue slipped out and licked the boy on his cheek. "Gotcha back," he whispered with a grin. Thus, began a quick rough and tumble - a boy and his, um, dog. "That was fun," he panted as they were joined by the rest of the troop.

"Come on, *Children*," Belinda groaned. "Cut it out. We have to find Sarah, before something happens to her."

"You take all the fun out of life, my dear. Please forgive us for taking the time for a bit of levity in this time of trial. Please?" Merlin sat up and extended a paw. "Let's be friends, okay?"

Belinda sighed and took the paw in her hand. "Okay, Merlin, but can we wait for playtime until after we rescue my sister?"

"Party pooper," the dog grumbled. "What's the harm in a little play, now and then?"

"Nothing, but there is a time and a place for everything, and this isn't the time, nor the place to—"

"Look out," Sure-shot whispered. "We have a dragon above us – a big black scaly dragon. "Don't look. Pretend you don't see her."

Belinda took a quick peek and whispered, "Maggie?"

"Sure looks like her. Don't pay any attention to her. If *she's* here, Sarah can't be far. I told you she was on the island."

"So, you did, my boy. So, you did. We must wait until the mighty dragon disappears, and then head in the direction she goes. Things are looking up. We will have Sarah back within the hour.

* * *

Something was wrong. She could feel it in her dragon bones. She scoured the countryside for any sign of trouble but found nothing. *My dragon instincts are never wrong. Something strange is happening, but what?* No one stirred, save for the shepherd's family tending their sheep. SHEEP! BREAKFAST! *The bacon must be a pile of ashes by now. Why did I leave without removing the pan from the stove? And the eggs*, she groaned. *The child will think me lax in my duties to her. I must hurry home.*

Normally, Maggie could have cared less for the comfort of anyone, other than herself, but she had grown rather fond of the young princess, and really did not wish her any harm. *Besides, if she starves to death, I will no longer have a hold over Hatchet. Who am I kidding? I must be getting soft.*

She turned and began to fly toward home. Breakfast must be completed and her family fed. Family? Yes. The only real family she had ever known. Family, who thought she was worthy of great things . . . a queen in her own right. *Bless the child. She seems to know me better than the family of my birth.*

Nothing, no, nothing must happen to our precious princess. She smiled a huge, but gentle, dragon smile, and flew as fast as she could toward home, to complete the morning meal. The child must be cared for properly.

* * *

"Um, Dad? Let's give it just another minute or two before we eat. I'm certain Maggie will be back any minute, and we don't want her to feel bad, do we?"

"Dautter, ye drives a hard bargain. But, if she be not arrivin' with five more minutes, kin we eat then? I'm most starved to death."

"Yes," Sarah giggled, "I can tell. But you better loosen your belt a bit, or nothing will fit in."

"Are ye sayin' I'm bein' fat, dautter?" he grumbled.

"Oh, no. I think you're perfect the way you are. But being a little careful will keep you looking slim and trim. I think Maggie would like it if you stayed slim and trim."

Hatchet sucked in his stomach. "Ye think so? She *is*

mighty beautiful, don't ye think?"

"She is indeed. And I know she likes you even if she likes to pretend she doesn't. And I think you like her, too."

Hatchet flushed. "Yer a smart one, ain't ye. I am bein' blessed with a dautter like you. But don't ye be tellin' anyone our little secret."

"What secret is that, Hatchet? You wouldn't be keeping something from me, would you?"

"Maggie!" Sarah jumped from her chair, bounded over to where the beautiful Maggie stood, and hugged her tightly.

Maggie stiffened from this unaccustomed affection and attempted to disengage the child's arms, but then thought better of it, and her arms slipped awkwardly around her young charge. "I'm happy to see you as well," she murmured. "But what is that wonderful smell? Hatchet? Did you complete breakfast for me?"

"No' I, but me dautter did it." He smiled proudly. "Smelled the bacon cookin', and saved the meal, with you being gone and all. Where were ye? It's not like yourself to be leaving anythin' unattended like. Ever'thin' all right?"

"Everything is perfect. Did you save anything for me?"

"Me dautter wouldn't let us eat 'til you was back. She didn't want t' seem impolite."

"Why, thank you, my darling girl." She smiled once

again at Sarah before settling at the table. "The bacon smells wonderful, and the eggs look delicious. Let's eat, shall we?"

Maggie was so impressed with her 'family' and what they had done for her, she failed to regard her dragon sense of danger.   But for now, the family meal was of utmost importance, and it had been prepared, with affection, by those she once thought the enemy. *Life is good.*

CHAPTER SIXTEEN

"Hey, she's gone. Where do you think she went?"

"Most likely to wherever Hatchet and Sarah are. Any ideas?" Merlin paused for a quick scratch.

"Most likely to the cave dwelling. It's the right direction, and she would feel safe there."

"Really, young knight. And why would you suggest the caverns rather than the mountains or forest . . . somewhere?"

"I've lived there, remember? Lots of hiding places, as well as escape routes. You should know that. You seem to know everything."

"Ah, yes. I see intelligence runs in your family. And you have the mind of a sleuth."

"What's a sleuth?" asked Anna, cocking her head slightly

"A sleuth, my dear, is a kind of detective. Someone who can figure out things maybe not so obvious to others. I assume you know, having lived your entire life on this island, just where this cave dwelling is. Yes?"

"Of course. I may be a shepherd girl, and an islander,

but I am not stupid. Besides, I've been there before. But the problem is not in getting to the caves, it's getting IN the caves . . to find Sarah, that is."

"That's true," murmured Sure-Shot. "Hatchet would just as soon cut off your head than allow anybody to enter the caves. Believe me, I know. If it wasn't for Grandpa, I'd probably be dead by now. But we've got to get in there someway just to make sure whether Sarah is in there or not. But how?"

"I'll go," Anna smiled shyly at Sure-shot.

"No!" Belinda bristled inside. "I'll go. After all, she's my sister."

"But she's my friend." Anna countered. "And I've been there before, so they wouldn't suspect anything." She smiled once more at Sure-Shot, who returned with a grateful smile of his own.

"I said *I'll* go. I'm responsible for Sarah, and she would expect me to rescue her." She glanced toward Sure-Shot, daring him to make the decision as to who was more suitable to rescue the young princess.

"Well . . . ." Sure-Shot stammered. "I—"

"Children, children. It has been decided that Brian, Todd and myself shall do the rescuing. Sorry, ladies, but you two, and the young knight, as willing as you may be, could easily be recognized, and perhaps captured as well. So, my dears, it is as it must be, I shall attempt the rescue, along with our excellent guide, Todd, and Brian, our willing fellow rescuer."

"That doesn't make sense. They know Brian and Todd as well as anybody." Belinda grumbled.

"Well, perhaps. But not as they shall see us, or not. It may not be original, but at least it's safer."

"What's safer?" Sure-Shot quizzed.

"Watch and learn," Merlin smiled. With a wave of his hand, Brian disappeared, and a scruffy orange cat stood in his place.

"Whoa . . ." gasped Belinda, as the cat rubbed against her jeans, purring loudly. "Uh, Brian? Is that you?" She picked up the cat and held him close. "I don't know if this is such a good idea. What if Maggie catches on and burns him to a crisp."

"Never fear, I would never let that happen, and besides Todd will be with us wherever we are."

"And Merlin dog," broke in Todd, "is being the greatest of all wizards. That dragon is being no match for the greatest of all wizards, no she is not. We shall find the small princess, yes, we will, and bring her home, safely. But we must be going, yes, we must. Darkness approaches."

"Todd is right, as usual. Sarah is in good hands, or at least she will be." Merlin woofed to make his point. "However, the day is half gone, so I suggest we give it one more day. Go back to the cottage, get some rest and begin anew at daylight. I'm sure Sarah will be just fine until then."

"How can you be so sure? What if she's being tortured, or something?"

"Maggie may be a dragon, but she has shown some small amount of wisdom in the past. It would be foolish of her to damage the goods, so to speak. What would she have to bargain with?"

"I don't like my sister being referred to as 'the goods'. It's so impersonal."

"My dear, child. It is merely a figure of speech. But Maggie may not see her as we do. To her, the child may just seem a means to an end. However, I am certain she is alright, and will remain so, at least for the near future. Tomorrow will come soon enough. These old bones need a bit of a rest before attempting a rescue. Let us go back to the cabin, have a good meal and rest a bit. Come, children, we must go . . . in the most expedient way."

With a wave of his paw, the rescuers disappeared, reappearing at the cabin door, anxious, but excited for the beginning of a new day."

* * *

Sarah . . . Sarah, dear. Would you mind coming here for just a moment? I have something important to discuss with you, if you would be so kind."

Sarah wiped her hands on a drying towel, folded it neatly and placed it on the drain board. Maggie had changed a lot during the weeks Sarah had been on the island, and the three of them appeared to be getting closer every day. She wondered what was so important that Maggie needed to talk to her now. With Hatchet out hunting for the evening meal, she supposed it was as good a time as any. Maggie didn't always like to have Hatchet privy to their conversations. And so, she hurried to the dinner table to find out what was on the dragon's mind. She settled next to her on the heavy metal bench and waited patiently for Maggie to begin. Finally, she spoke.

"Sarah, dear. I've been thinking. I know we've talked a lot about my beloved and his . . . um . . . human mate, and you tell me how much he loves her, and she him. But I am confused. He told me he loved me. He saved my life, and I owe my life to him. But I am confused and curious about this 'wife' of his. I know he could not possibly love her more than me, but I would like to know more about her . . . to try to understand, you see. I have a proposition for you.

"If I could just observe her with my own eyes, even from a distance, and see if she is really what she seems to be, perhaps I could learn to live a solitary life, without him, If I could ascertain that she is truly worthy of his love, and that she truly loves him as I do. I do not think it possible, but on the other hand, it does appear that he is smitten with her, and I do wish him all happiness. You do understand, do you not, my child?"

Sarah squirmed in her seat. This was not like Maggie, and she wondered for just a moment what Maggie was up to, but then dismissed it from her mind. Maggie was confiding in her and Sarah did want to help her if she could. "Explain to me a little bit more, please. Now, I'm a little confused. Don't you want him anymore?"

"Of course, I do," Maggie snapped, then softened. "It's just that I want his happiness as well. I know he loves me, but he loves her as well. I wish to see her with my own eyes, perhaps speak to her to ascertain whether she truly is one I can trust my love to, or whether she is an imposter and would do more harm than good to the one I love."

"Whoa, are you serious?"

"Immensely so. I do love him and want his happiness above all, you know."

"Wow, that's great. But are you sure?"

"Of course, I'm sure. But I do need your help, just a bit."

"Well, what can *I* do to help?"

"Well, my dear. I need you to contact Max, through Rocky, and have him contact Magdalyn and tell her I wish to let you go home, but only if she comes to the painting and takes you out herself. You see dear, I have no way to let you through the painting into the great room. Only someone from the outside can get through to the inside, and thus help you to reach the great room safely. I have been forbidden to access the room, so I cannot set you free. However, she must come alone, telling no one of her quest. I cannot be seen. I just wish to observe. Then I can send you home and be content. You do understand, do you not?"

"I think so, but what do you know about Rocky and Max."

"Oh, my child, I have always known. My beloved, himself, told me about this way of communication with his boy. And this is how *we* will communicate, until I can see her for myself, and," she paused with a sigh, "can then live my life without him, if necessary, knowing all will be well with my beloved. However, child, no one else can be privy to this information. I am putting my life on the line by letting you go. If someone should see me, I am certain they would not hesitate to kill me, not knowing my good intentions, rather than listen to reason. Humans are not a reasonable people."

"What about, um, Dad? Can I let him know? He'll be really upset if he finds me gone without saying good-bye."

"I'm afraid not, my dear. He might slip and say something, and that would be the end of me. You don't want to see me killed, do you?"

"Of course not. You're my friend. I would never want to see you killed. But are you sure about everything? Won't you miss me . . . even a little bit?"

"Of course, I will miss you, but you did promise to visit once in a while, did you not? It's not like you'll be gone forever."

"No, I guess not. But I will really miss you." Sarah threw her arms around the huge dragon and squeezed her tightly. "Thank you, Maggie. I love you, and I'll miss you . . . and Dad too, but I promise I'll be back for a visit as often as I can."

"And don't forget, child. You must mention this to no one. All our lives depend on it. Come, we have things to do, things to prepare. Remember your promise. Shhh, someone's coming. Sounds like Hatchet with our evening meal. Remember, tell no one of our plans . . . not even Hatchet. He may not approve," she murmured. "You must go to Rocky. We must begin planning your return home."

CHAPTER SEVENTEEN

"Rocky . . . Rocky . . . I'm going home. Can you believe it?"

"Wonderful, small princess. Tell me all about it. When are you going, and will you take me with you? I would like to see my brother. What shall I wear? What shall I pack? Is it a long trip? Do you think Max will be glad to see me . . . and Robert, and the boy? I'm so happy."

"Um, Rocky. I hate to break this to you, but I don't think you can come with me. But you *can* talk to Max. I need to get a message to Magdalyn right away."

"Humph," Rocky sobbed. "Why am I always left behind? Am I that intolerable no one wants me around? I am loathed, unwanted. Why? Why, does everyone hate me so? I never get to go anywhere, do anything . . . but sit on this uncomfortable shelf, day after day, bored stiff."

"Rocky, you're stiff because you're made of stone. And I love you. I wish I could take you with me, but you need to stay here and be Robert's eyes and ears. He needs you. We all need you. So, will you please get a message to Max so he can tell Magdalyn to contact you so that I can get the message to her, so I can go home. I will come back for you if I can, I mean *when* I can."

"Do you promise you'll come back? Do you really love me? Really truly?" He sighed deeply.

"Of course, I do. Really truly. What's not to love? Now, can you get a message to Max? Ask him to have Magdalyn call in one hour, if he can. And make sure he knows not to say anything to anyone else and tell him to tell Magdalyn it's a secret and not to tell anyone, not even Alfred."

Rocky stared at the child for just a moment, one eyebrow cocked, a light bit of confusion on his face. "That does not seem quite right . . . to keep a secret from one's other half. Do you not think?"

"But it's important. It's to be a big surprise, and we don't want to ruin it."

"A surprise?" Rocky bubbled. "Like a surprise birthday party?"

"Well, yes, kinda, only better. And I can leave as soon as we make the arrangements. I get to go home. Isn't that exciting?" She hesitated at Rocky's sad expression. "But . . . I will miss you, and 'Dad' and everyone. And I will be back, sooner than you know it. You'll hardly have time to miss me."

"I miss you, already. But tell me, small princess, what

will the dragon say if you are suddenly gone?"

"It was her idea. She just wants to see what Magdalyn looks like, then I can go home. She wants me to go home."

"Humph." Rocky bristled. "I think you had best think this over, small princess. That black demon thinks of no one but herself, and there must be a reason to benefit her, if she is willing to let you go. I would think this over, if I were you."

"Oh, Rocky. Don't be silly. I'll be okay. Besides, she made a solemn promise. Everything is going to work out just fine. She's changed . . . she really has. She is much nicer now. And I trust her to do what's right." Sarah's stubborn chin spoke volumes, as her eyes narrowed.

"I hope you are right, small princess. But . . . she has been known to lie, to get what she wants. Just be careful and watch your back. Promise?"

"I promise, but I don't think she'd lie to me. She says Hatchet and me are her family, and family doesn't lie to each other!"

"Well . . . yes. I see what you mean. You are family to me, and I must protect my small princess. From herself, if necessary," he whispered to himself.

"Then you'll call Max for me?"

"I will call my brother." Rocky sighed. "I will let you know when I hear from him. You just be careful. And small princess, never trust anyone at face value. Always watch your back and be careful. I will miss you greatly. And don't forget who your true friends are. We who truly love you." The golem sniffed loudly, as Sarah threw her arms around him and hugged him tight.

"I won't forget . . . and don't you forget either. I will be back. Then maybe I can take you to see the outside world. Would you like that?"

"Ah, 'twould be Heaven to not be forgotten, and to see new places never before experienced. Hurry now, sweet princess. You must go and prepare for your journey. I will say a prayer for your safe return."

"Thank you, Rocky. Call me when you reach Max or Magdalyn. You take care of yourself while I'm gone. You hear?" She grinned. "Gotta go. I'm so excited. Don't forget, call me, as soon as—"

"Yes, yes. As soon as I reach Max, I will call."

"Bye, Rocky. It won't take me long to get ready, so try to hurry. Love you." And she was gone.

Ah, child. I hope you are correct in your perceptions. The black demon dragon is not to be trusted. I pray for your safe return. Minutes later, his task was completed, and he waited pensively for Max to return his call. This could take a while.

Slowly, the golem returned to his natural state, stiff, and hard as the stone from which he had been made, forcing his tears to remain at bay.

CHAPTER EIGHTEEN

"Maggie . . . Maggie . . .   she's coming. Magdalyn's coming. And she said she wouldn't tell anyone."

"That's wonderful!" Maggie grinned a toothy dragon grin. "It is time I observed my rival . . . I mean, my beloved's . . . um . . . human wife, the other woman, so to speak, and make proper judgement as to her worthiness in his life."

"Maggie?" Sarah scrutinized the huge dragon. "You *are* just going to observe . . . right? You're not going to do anything stupid are you? If you're even thinking about it, I'm not going, and I'll tell her not to come, either."

"Child, child. You know me by now. Would I ever lie to you . . . my adopted daughter? Now what kind of a mother would I be, lying to my favorite child? My intentions are pure. I promise. I see this . . . woman . . . wife, and then you can go home as promised." ***When I am ready for you to go.*** "Oh, what a glorious day it will be. Perhaps I will even be able to forgive my beloved for his indiscretion." *He may be 'married' to her, but he belongs to me.* "Ah, yes. We shall soon see what we shall see. Come child, we need to prepare."

* * *

Merlin slowly crept along the edge of an outcropping over-looking the cave dwelling, where Sarah was no doubt suffering at the hands of the evil dragon and her henchman. Brian, transformed into a disheveled cat, crept along behind Merlin, while Todd waited not-so-patiently for instructions.

"There it is," Merlin whispered.

"Okay," the scruffy cat bounced in anxious energy, "Is it time to attack? Um . . . well, you know what I mean."

"I do indeed. But be patient, my son, there is movement at the entrance. We must wait until all is clear. It will not do to be seen before the time is right. Merlin sat in the shadows and watched as the two figures exited the cave dwelling. He cocked his head to one side. *This is an interesting change of events. The small princess looks interestingly happy, but who is that striking black woman with her?* "Stop!" Merlin whispered loudly and held out a paw as the cat tried to slink past.

"But it's Sarah. We've got to save her."

"She does not appear to be in peril, at the moment, and if we rush them there could be— Brian! Get back here!" But Brian was past hearing as he raced toward his young friend.

* * *

"Come, child, we must hurry if we are to meet this woman, this *wife* of my beloved, lest she tire and leave before we get to our rendezvous point. It will not do to miss our . . . our meeting. I uh. . . will miss you greatly, my daughter. You will not forget me, will you?"

"You know I could never forget you, Maggie. I, um, love both you and Dad. I could never forget you. But you're right, we must hurry. It's getting late, and Magdalyn might worry if we don't show up on time. But . . . don't forget . . . you can look at her, but you cannot let her see you. You promised. And I will be back to visit. I promise."

"Wonderful, my child. Now climb aboard. We must be off." Maggie quickly morphed into the black dragon and extended one massive wing. Sarah scrambled up the wing, making herself comfortable on Maggie's upper back, locking her feet in the tight grooves where the dragon wings flexed for flight. As soon as Sarah was safely settled, Maggie spread her wings and with a mighty whoosh, lifted off the ground and took to the skies.

"Whoa, did you see that?" The scruffy cat plopped to the ground, his mouth opened in wonder and awe. "They act like they're best friends. What gives?"

"Yes," Merlin muttered. "What gives, indeed?" He sat

next to the cat and stared after the duo as they disappeared from sight. *Something is not right here. Not right at all.*

* * *

Maggie watched from the shadows, as her human daughter stood patiently, scrutinizing the great room for any sign of Magdalyn. But the room was empty. With tears in her eyes, Sarah turned and searched the dark forest for her dragon mother, spotting her a few feet down the road, behind an enormous evergreen stand. She shrugged her shoulders, and tried to smile, in spite of the no show, and the knowledge she would never be able to go home. Maggie smiled back sympathetically but grated inside.

Just as she started to call Sarah to come to her, the door opened, Magdalyn cautiously peered into the room, and silently stepped through, carefully shutting the door behind her. Spotting Sarah in the castle painting, she rushed to greet her.

Sarah leaned toward the barrier but was stopped by the magic protecting the great room from the painting's inhabitants. Placing both hands on the painting, she pushed slightly . . . just in case. Magdalyn stood in front of the painting and stared at Sarah, with joy in her eyes. "Oh, my darling girl. You're alright. We have been so worried. Come, my dear. We must let your parents know you have arrived."

"I—I can't get through. Maggie says the barrier is too strong, so you have to reach in to get me and pull me through."

"Oh, of course. I am so excited to see you, safe and sound. Give me your hand." Magdalyn stuck her hand through the barrier and grabbed Sarah's extended hand. But as she began to pull, a strong vine flew in from the forest and twisted around both of the human's wrists Magdalyn found herself pulled through the painting and onto the forest pathway. "What?" she startled. "W-where am I?"

Maggie pulled on the vine, dragging the two closer to her.

"Maggie? What are you doing?" Sarah cried. "You promised!"

"Indeed, I did, my daughter. And I will keep my promise. However, I am not yet ready to fulfill that promise. I need time to determine what is to be done and when. In other words, this person will be mine until I decide to let her go. I must get to know her . . . to know why my beloved chose her over me. She must be a witch to have deceived him into leaving the one he truly loves for a mere mortal. She will come with me . . . until I decide otherwise."

"You're a liar! I hate you. You promised!" Sarah
screamed as Maggie grabbed Magdalyn and flexed her
wings to take flight. Remarkably, Magdalyn didn't protest,
but hung limply in Maggie's arms.

"I'm sorry you feel that way, but it was a necessary
ruse. Would you have agreed if I had told you my true
intentions? No, so I had to do it my way . . . or I might
never know. Do you understand, my daughter? It is for the
best.

"Are you coming? Climb aboard, quickly, if you are of
a mind, or you can stay here and hope to be rescued. I would
remind you, however, the dark forest is full of danger, and
there is no promise of rescue. So, either come or stay. It is of
no consequence for the eventual outcome."

Sarah bristled inside but knew, for Magdalyn's sake,
she had to do as Maggie said, at least for the time being.
Magdalyn was in this mess because of her, and she must at
least try to rescue her friend. Or, if nothing else, try to
protect her and give her someone to talk to if the going got
too tough. "I'm coming," she scowled. "But I'm not happy
about it. I will never forget what you've done. And I will
never forgive you." She scrambled up Maggie's extended
wing and settled unhappily in her usual position. "Are you
going to carry her all the way to the island? Don't you think

it would be better if she rode with me?

"I will carry her as long as I can, she weighs little, it appears, then I will allow her to join you before we cross the great ocean. Does that meet with your approval, my daughter?"

"I am *not* the daughter of a liar. But I will accept your offer, if you are not lying to me again. Dad would be so disappointed in you."

Maggie cringed inside. "It matters not. I am the maker of decisions, and I will decide what is right, and when to change my mind, or not. I am sorry you feel the way you do, but it is an unfortunate necessity. So, learn to live with it. I will not harm her, unless she provokes me." She spread her wings and rose to the skies. It hurt her to see her 'daughter' so upset, and her words about Hatchet . . . well, enough said. Her mind was in a whirl as she set course for the island. *She will understand, someday.*

CHAPTER NINETEEN

"We can't leave yet. We haven't got Sarah, and I can't go home without my sister." Belinda snapped, near tears.

"My darling girl," Merlin soothed, "At this point, we don't even know where she is. Besides, I don't think she is in any danger. Me thinks Maggie is perhaps in greater danger than Sarah. We watched them leave and Maggie seemed to have a genuine affection for our girl, and Sarah didn't stop talking until they were out of sigh, if then."

"I don't care! I said I would bring her home, and I intend to do it." With arms across her chest, Belinda glared at those around her."

"I think the best course of action would be to go home and consult with the others about the best course of action. Besides, Brian needs to see his grandmother again. I'm sure he misses her greatly."

"Brian, or you?" giggled Anna.

"Well," hedged Merlin. "I must confess, I might miss her just a bit. Besides, she makes a mean Chicken and Dumplings." He patted his stomach. "I feel I am beginning to waste away to nothing. A lovely woman, our Gwenny. Come, we must get back to the mansion, have something to eat, and then . . . who knows? Maybe some dessert?

"It serves no purpose to remain on the island. Especially when we know not when they will return. For all we know, Sarah could already be home. I'm certain Da and his family will be glad to inform us, should they return to the island."

"Of course, of course," Da agreed. "Perhaps it would be best to return to your homes. We will let you know if we find out anything. Anna will keep a close eye on the mountain and the sky. We *will* find her if she returns to the island, Now, you must do as Merlin says. We will see you soon. Now you must go. We look forward to seeing you again. May the Great Creator be with you all and bring you back safely. Now, let me show you to the door."

"Thank you," Merlin whispered, as he ushered his troop to the door.

"If it is being alright with our great wizard, Todd will stay and continue to search for the small princess, with the beautiful Anna, yes I will. We will find her, yes we will."

So, it was agreed. As soon as the would-be rescuers gathered outside of the cabin, Merlin waved his arm and they found themselves back in the great room to face the worried family, minus one.

* * *

Alfred frantically rushed through the mansion, as fast as his elderly legs could take him. "Magdalyn . . . Magdalyn . . . . where are you?"

"Alfred?" Bee Lewis slipped down the staircase, with Gwenny close behind. "Whatever is the matter? And why are you not in the great room? You know what Merlin said."

"Indeed, I do, my lady. But I have searched everywhere, and I cannot find her."

"Find who?" interjected Gwenny "What are you caterwauling about?"

"Magdalyn, my beloved, has disappeared. I cannot find her anywhere. I have searched the house from top to bottom, but she is nowhere to be found.

"Could she have gone into the gardens, or out to the kennel to see the pups?" Bee was beginning to panic.

"She knows to never leave the great room, much less the house. I fear something dire may have happened to her."

"Where would she go? There's no place for her *to* go, unless . . . ."

"Unless what?" Alfred asked.

Gwenny stared at Bee, concern in her eyes. "You don't suppose?"

"I-I don't know. It's possible. But why would she do that? She knows the danger."

"Why would she do what?" Alfred demanded.

"Alfred, dear." Bee linked her arm with Alfred's and asked, "You don't suppose she went off to look for Sarah on her own, do you?"

"Absolutely not." Alfred bristled. "She knows the danger. Besides, she would tell me if she even thought about doing something so . . .. so . . . ."

"Stupid?" Gwenny filled in the blanks.

"My wife is *not* stupid. She is the most intelligent woman I know. Along with, of course, you two lovely ladies. I—"

"Of course, she is," soothed Bee. "But she has to be somewhere. Do you have any idea, any idea at all, where she might have got herself off to?" One look at Alfred's terrified features and Bee knew not to inquire further. "Come," she ordered. "To the great room. We must call Merlin. If she did indeed find her way into the painting, Merlin would know. He is our only hope. We must hurry." *Merlin . . . Merlin . . .* Bee silently pleaded. *We need you. Come home now. Magdalyn is missing. Wherever you are, come home.*

As one, the three raced to the great room, in hopes it

was not already too late.

* * *

Merlin stood and stretched a mighty stretch before turning to his comrades. "Well, how do I look, now that I'm back to my natural self?" He shook out his robes and dusted off his pointed star-incrusted hat.

"You look wonderful, Merlin. Just as good as new . . . um . . . as old." She giggled.

Sure-shot quickly gave him the once-over, and said, "I kinda liked you as a dog. You were pretty cool."

"Why, thank you, son, but I think I prefer my usual self – a lot less fleas." He chuckled, scratching briefly behind his left ear to prove his point. "Brian, my boy, what do you think?"

But Brian was saved from answering, as the great room door flew open, and three worried individuals flew through the door.

"Grandpa . . . Aunt Gwenny . . . Mrs. Bee. What's wrong?"

Gwenny ran to Merlin and hugged him tightly. "Oh, thank the Good Lord you have returned."

"Well, I'm glad to see you, too," Merlin smiled, patting her gently on her shoulder. "But I sense something a bit more than that you're glad to see us. What's been going on while we were, um . . . otherwise occupied?"

"First of all, did you find Sarah?" Grandma Bee asked.

"Well, yes and no," Merlin hedged.

"What does that mean? You either did, or you didn't."

"Well, technically we did find her, but she didn't see us. That black dragon was in the process of spiriting her off somewhere, so we came home to put our heads together to try to determine where they might have gone off to. Now, what is the problem here?"

"My wife has disappeared," Alfred broke in, "and we can't find her anywhere. We were wondering if she might have gone into the Castle Painting, on her own, to try to find Sarah. Did you see her there?"

"Unfortunately, no. But that doesn't mean she is not there. It could be that Maggie lured her to the painting, using Sarah as the bait, so to speak, and kidnapped her then."

"What makes you think so, Merlin? Did they say something, do something to lead you to that conclusion?" Gwenny squeezed his forearm as tightly as she dared.

"Not really. We were too far away to hear anything. We couldn't let them know we were there, you see. But there didn't appear to be anything untoward going on." Merlin paused and stroke his beard, his eyes unfocused in thoughtful silence. "However, it's quite possible, if but improbable.

"Perhaps that is why they seemed to be in such a hurry, but Sarah did look happy. If she thought she was coming home, or would have a human companion, to wile away the time, it's possible the black demon could have persuaded her to help her in this diabolical conquest . . .. However, it is just as possible that we are grasping at straws.

We need to contact Lord Henry, just to see if he has heard of anything going on. Come, we need to talk. Let's go someplace quiet, where we can confer, and perhaps have a bite to eat? What do you think, my lady?" Merlin smiled gently at Gwenny and she smiled back. "Do you think you could manage to come up with something delicious for a starving Wizard and his crew?" He patted the hand still gripping his arm.

"Oh." Embarrassed, Gwenny loosened her grip, and then dropped his arm, like the proverbial hot potato. "Right away, sir. I have Chicken and Dumplings already cooked and ready to eat. Would that suffice, my lord?"

"Yummm." Merlin licked his lips. "That would more than suffice, my dear." He took her hand in his, and lightly kissed her fingertips. "'Twould be Heaven, to a starving man's palate. We have greatly missed your excellent fare."

Blushing profusely, Gwenny extracted her hand, and fled toward the great room door. Just before passing through, she looked back and said, "Dinner will be served in ten minutes, or less. I will meet you *all* in the dining room in a timely manner. Be there, ready to eat."

"What a delightful woman," Merlin murmured to himself, then said out loud, "Has anyone seen Professor Hawthorn? We will need him for this quest."

CHAPTER TWENTY

Maggie landed, as gently as she could, at the cave entrance and glanced at the riders still clinging to her back, *Good, we hadn't lost anyone* - although she had been tempted to dislodge the irritating Magdalyn. Lying flat on the ground, she extended her wing, and waited for her rival and her 'daughter' to descend.

Sarah dismounted first and then helped Magdalyn to disembark. Stomping past Maggie, with Magdalyn close behind, she turned and whispered loudly. "You're a liar, and I don't know if I can ever forgive you."

Maggie fought back a dragon tear, her mind a whirl. Her intentions had been honorable, but when she saw her rival, for the first time, she was obsessed with hatred for this person, but the woman seemed different than she had imagined, and now she wasn't certain what to think about this woman, her beloved's human wife. *I must think this through, get to know this person a bit before making final judgement.* Glancing once more at the pair entering the cavern, she stretched her wings and flew away. *I must think about all this mess.*

Magdalyn turned and watched as the black dragon flew toward the forest edge, and pity filled her soul. She knew what it was like to truly love someone, and if Maggie felt only a quarter of what she felt for her husband, she must love him more than even he knew. Her heart softened, and she felt truly sorry for the dragon. Truly sorry.

* * *

"Dautter! Ye 'ave returned. I thought you was gone forever. I'm that happy to be seein' you again, that I am." He turned his attention to Magdalyn, and his eyes narrowed. And who be this," he muttered. "Another mouth t' feed, I wager. It's most dinner time, and I'm doing me best to fix somethin' to eat. How am I gonna fix somethin' for four people? It's just not right. No, it ain't," he grumbled.

"Perhaps I could be of service, sir?" Magdalyn smiled at the outlaw. "If you don't mind, that is. I am known to be a fair cook in my own right. I would be happy to assist you, if you would be needing my services."

"You, bein' a real lady, would be willin' to help someone like me? I don't know. The great dragon, Maggie, would say, I am not worthy of yer help . . . but if ye would like to lend a hand, I guess I *could* use a little help."

"Dad, you have got to stop putting yourself down. You

are most wonderful, and a lot better than that lying dragon. She's the one who is unworthy of you."

"Dautter, you don't know what you are sayin'. Maggie is very powerful, and dangerous, too. Be careful, dautter, I don't want no harm to come to ye. Never!"

"Sarah, dear. Why does this man call you daughter? Your father is home in the real world. And this man is certainly not your father."

"Hatchet *is* my dad while I am on the island. We have a pretty good relationship and he protects me from all the bad stuff. And besides, we're good friends, aren't we, Dad."

"Oh, I think I understand. Sarah, dear, if this 'dad' means that much to you, he must be a good person. So," she addressed Hatchet," it will be my pleasure to assist you in any way, sir."

"The pleasure be mine, yer ladyship." Hatchet smiled as big a smile as he could muster and said. "But if we be going to get dinner ready afore Maggie gets back, we had best get movin'. Foller me, your ladyship."

"Hatchet? I would really like it if you called me Magdalyn. If I'm going to be here for a while, I am just one of the gang. Do you mind if I call you Hatchet?"

Hatchet beamed. "'twould be my pleasure, your ladyship, um, I mean Magdalyn, ma'am."

Magdalyn took Hatchet's arm and smiled. "You, sir, are a true gentleman. It is *my* pleasure to meet *you*. Shall we go?" She turned and smiled at Sarah. "Come, Sarah, dear? Your 'Dad' needs some assistance in the kitchen."

Sarah watched as the lady and the outlaw sauntered arm in arm toward the kitchen and smiled a perplexed smile. *Who knew? Magdalyn truly is a lady. This might work out after all.*

* * *

Maggie watched from the shadows as the trio talked and laughed while preparing the evening meal. Her eyes narrowed and she suddenly grew disturbed at this easy comradery. *What is it with this woman? Must she have every man eating out of her hand? First my beloved, and now Hatchet. Even my new daughter seems smitten with her. This bears some looking into.* She turned and walked slowly toward the room at the far end of the hall.

CHAPTER TWENTY-ONE

Maggie pursed her lips, applied some scarlet lip rouge, and rubbed her lips together. *There, that looks sufficient.* She smacked her lips, with a popping sound, and quickly applied color to her eyelids. *How do they do this? she* sighed. *It doesn't look quite right, but I am indeed beautiful, am I not? At least to human standards.* She sighed, threw on a lovely print dress and, in her human body, sauntered to the eating area for dinner. She hesitated, for just a moment, before entering, then swept in, waiting for someone, anyone, to notice her beauty and compliment her on her new look.

"M-Maggie? Is that you?" Sarah choked. "You look, um . . . different."

"Why, thank you, child. Did I do it right?"

But before Sarah could answer, Hatchet burst into laughter, then quickly hid his face, doing his best to hide even a hint of a smile.

"Hatchet," Maggie demanded. "Look at me. Do I not look lovely? Hatchet! Look—at—me! I wish to know what you think."

"Beg pardon, yer 'ighness, but . . . ." The outlaw stole a quick peek at the 'beauteous' woman standing before him, and once again burst into fits of laughter.

"What is wrong with him, daughter?" Maggie asked, puzzled by his reaction. She had tried so hard, and this is the thanks she got.

"Hatchet?" Magdalyn broke in gently.

"Yes, ma'am."

"You appear to be impolite to our benefactor. This is not a laughing matter." Suppressing a smile, she continued. "Maggie has tried very hard to make herself presentable to the family, and we need to respect her efforts. Do you not agree."

"I agree," bubbled Sarah.

"Thank you, dear," smiled Magdalyn, "but I was asking for Hatchet's opinion. Hatchet? What say you?"

"But she be lookin' like a lady o' the night."

"W-what?" Maggie startled, confused tears filling her eyes. This was not how she expected to be perceived, and her heart was shattered. "I-I guess I should go," She grabbed a napkin and began to scrub at the makeup she had so carefully applied.

"Maggie, dear," Magdalyn hurried to intercept. "Hatchet didn't mean that to sound the way it did." She smiled slightly at Hatchet before turning back to Maggie.

"However, dear, if you don't mind my saying so, I think that although you are indeed beautiful, your makeup might be a bit too much for a casual dinner at home. I'm sure Hatchet is thinking, that you look more suitable to be going out for the evening. Isn't that what you meant, Hatchet, sir?"

Hatchet gulped, suddenly contrite. "Um, yes, ma'am. That be exactly right. A lovely woman . . . for a lovely night out on the town." He smiled as brightly as he could. Maggie returned a grateful smile.

Sarah stared at Magdalyn. *Wow, you are good, Magdalyn. No wonder everybody loves you.*

"Maggie, dear. You seem to be new at this sort of thing. Not that you don't do it quite well, for a first time. But . . . I was wondering, if it is alright with you, of course, if you would mind a few pointers, from the human point of view, for daytime use of facial color. I would be glad to assist you, it you so desire."

"Can you help me?" Sarah begged. "I want to be beautiful."

"In time, dear one. But for now, I think we should leave the makeup for the women of the household. Do you not think, dear?"

"I guess," sulked Sarah. "But when I get older?"

"Yes, dear. When you are older, I will teach you what I can. But for now, it's Maggie's turn. That is, if she wishes to learn."

Maggie stared at Magdalyn with some skepticism. "I am . . . in . . . agreement, if you are not trying to trick me. Can you really make me look beautiful?"

"You are already beautiful, Maggie. However, I can always try to teach you how to enhance that beauty, if you so desire."

Maggie cocked her head. "Do you really think I'm . . . beautiful . . . as beautiful as you?" Her eyes narrowed and she watched with curious interest what Magdalyn's answer would be."

"Even more so. And I have often heard Alfred speak of your great beauty."

"Really? Did he really, truly say so? I knew he loved me," she murmured softly.

"Yes, Maggie, dear. Alfred does love you, but in a different way. And he loves me, as well. You are his favorite dragon friend. I am merely his wife. But I can assure you, he loves us both, but in different ways. Do you understand?"

"Hmmm. I shall think on this," Maggie spoke thoughtfully. "In the meantime, we should eat, and then we can talk beauty treatments, if you . . . are still . . . willing."

"Of course, I am. We can start tomorrow. But now, let's eat. I'm starving." She smiled broadly and seated herself at the iron table. *This is so exciting. I think I may have found a new friend. Old enemy . . . new friend. Yes! . . . . I hope . . ..*

CHAPTER TWENTY-TWO

The Winthrop Mansion was in turmoil. It had been several days since the lovely Magdalyn had disappeared, and Alfred was distraught, driving the household crazy with his anguish. Sarah was momentarily relegated to secondary status as concern for Magdalyn grew to momentous proportions.

"Alfred, you must calm down. Driving everyone crazy is not going to get Magdalyn back. I'm sure she's fine and probably having the time of her life."

"With all due respect, Bee, you don't know Maggie like I do. She could be torturing my beloved. She could be starving her to death, or any other means of torment." He paused, for just a moment, quickly scanning the great room. "What is that infernal noise?" With that the howling increased significantly.

"It's all my fault. It's all my fault." Max sobbed, tears leaving rivulets of melting clay down his remorseful cheeks.

"What are you talking about? What's your fault?"

"She made me promise. I wanted to tell, but she made

me promise. I am bad, so, so, bad. I should be thrown into the river and drowned, or at least melted away. I am so sorry. Why did I listen to her?"

"Listen to whom?" Bee asked, great concern in her eyes for this tiny being.

"The lady . . . the lady Magdalyn. She made me promise not to tell. But I didn't know . . . I didn't know." He began to bawl even louder.

Alfred snatched the golem from his grandson's hands and snarled at the tiny figure. "What are you sniveling about? And what do you know about my beloved?"

"It was the young princess's idea. She told my brother, Rocky, to tell me not to tell, that she needed to talk to our lady, right away, because it was an emergency, and then I had to give the message to Magdalyn, and I wanted to warn you, but she said everything would be alright, and that if she went, and didn't tell anyone, the young princess would be returned, and everything would be alright. But now she's gone . . . gone . . . both of them . . . are gone, and it's all my fault. I'm so sorry." The golem began to weep once again.

"You knew, and you didn't tell me?!"

"But she made me promise. I couldn't break a promise, could I?"

Alfred raised the terrified golem high into the air and

prepared to smash him into the nearest wall.

"Help!" screamed Max. "Help! Murder . . . Murder. Please. Someone . . . anyone . . . save me. I don't want to die."

Bee grabbed Alfred's arm and gently, but firmly, extracted the golem from the hands of the angry wizard.

"Alfred! Calm yourself! If you smash Max, we may never be able to communicate with Magdalyn again."

"W-what?" He stared at the golem for just a moment, and then buried his head in his hands. "What am I doing? Forgive me, Max. I wasn't thinking. I'm so worried. Tell, me, my friend, what do you know about the whereabouts of my beloved, and how can we be assured of her return?"

Max was tempted to give a snarky response but hesitated at the horror still etched on Alfred's face. Softening, the golem murmured. "I am certain the lady is alive and well. If it were otherwise, Rocky would certainly have told me. He is very good at things like that. Perhaps I could arrange a time for you to speak with the lady. Would you like that?"

"Can you do that? I would be forever grateful."

"I can certainly try. There is no guarantee, but I know Rocky is just as concerned, and would do his best to comply, if possible. I will contact him immediately."

"Thank you, Max. If you can do this, I will be eternally grateful."

"You won't try to smash me again?"

"Never. You are my friend, and you are my creation, if you will remember."

"*I* remember," Max huffed. "Just make certain that *you* do. If Master Sure-Shot will take me to our room, I will attempt to contact my brother and find out when the rendezvous can take place. Agreed?"

"Agreed. Thank you, Max. You're a good man . . . um, golem. I look forward to our next communication." He reached out to pat the golem on his stone head, but Max quickly dodged and raised a hand to prevent the endearment.

"Please do not touch my being. Your hands are damp, and I do not want to expire before my time." Max grinned at the confused wizard. Shifting his stone body toward Sure-Shot he said, "Come, boy. We must hurry. We must contact my brother." Then lowering his voice to a whisper, he added, *"before it is too late,"*

* * *

"I'm not certain exactly how to get started, Maggie. You are certainly limited on beauty products. You have . . .um . . . lovely skin, but I will have to guess at what will look best as your color scheme."

"Does it matter?" Maggie snapped. "Just make me beautiful. Is that too much to ask?"

Magdalyn frowned, stepped back a pace or two, and with her arms folded across her chest, stared at the dragon, (now human . . . at least for the time being.)

"What's the matter? Why aren't you working?"

"Maggie, dear. I think while we are doing your makeover, we should concentrate, as well, on your attitude. If you want humans, dragons, or otherwise, as the case may be, to treat you with the dignity you deserve, we have a lot of work to do."

"What do you mean?" Maggie growled. "My attitude is exemplary. Ask anyone."

"Maggie! Look at me!"

Against her better judgement, Maggie slowly turned and stared at Magdalyn with eyes half closed. "Yes?"

Magdalyn sighed, and gently lifted Maggie's chin until they were eye-to-eye. "Maggie, dear. Do you want my help, or not? I can have you send me back home, if you are not satisfied with my attempts with your beauty treatments . . . or at becoming your friend. I'm sure Alfred would understand." She smiled as sweetly as she dared.

"No! I will not allow it. You will stay until *I* decide you will go. And do not speak thus of my master," she barked, her eyes flashing. But almost immediately her demeanor softened, and she spoke in a chastised tone. "Please forgive me. I am not myself today," she purred, smooth as silk.

"As you, wish, dear. Now, I am going to apply some simple foundation. Watch carefully, as when I am through, I will wipe it all off, and you can try it for yourself. Will that be acceptable to you, Maggie dear?" Magdalyn picked up a small container of some kind of . . . moisturizer? She grimaced, but then tentatively pulled out two fingers full of goo. "Here we go," she smiled.

A few minutes later, Maggie was applying her own layer of goo. "Did I do it right?" she asked.

"You did it beautifully. Now we'll try the foundation." Within the hour, Maggie made several attempts at putting on her own makeup, and Magdalyn, at last, proclaimed she was now somewhat proficient at her own beauty care. "Well, Maggie, shall we go in to lunch and see what the others think about the new you?"

"Oh, yes," Maggie agreed, Let's go." Peering at her reflection from all angles, she smiled to herself. *I am indeed beautiful.* "Thank you . . . . Magdalyn. Let us see how they see me now." She rose, and stepping as regally as she could, walked toward the door, Magdalyn close behind.

* * *

Hatchet starred at the lovely black woman as she waltzed through the door, his heart skipping a quick beat.

"Wow, Maggie, is it really you? You look like — wow."

"Thank you, child. Your approval means a great deal to me." She responded to Sarah, but her questioning eyes were on the man gripping the ladle, standing by the stove. But Hatchet was too awed to say a word.

"Hatchet," Magdalyn smiled. "What do you think?" She gestured toward Maggie.

"Um . . . I . . . um."

"Hatchet, it's okay. Maggie would just like to know whether you approve of her new look. That's all." She glanced toward Maggie, tears forming in the corners of the woman/dragon's eyes.

Maggie's heart was broken at the seeming indifference of one she was beginning to care for. "Well, my dears." She tried to appear brave and nonchalant. "I'm not really all that hungry. But I am very tired. It's been a big day, and I think I will retire." She turned and fled to her room.

"You are most beautiful," Hatchet called after her, but she was long past hearing.

Shutting and securely locking her door, she dropped onto her bed and covered her head, large salty droplets dripping down her cheeks. *Alfred . . . my Alfred . . . you would never treat me thus. I need to see you. Prove to you that I am the one you love. Magdalyn appears to be a lovely person, but I know I am your true love. I will find a way to come to you . . . I will. Then we can be together. . . forever.* And so, a plan was formed as she drifted off to sleep.

CHAPTER TWENTY-THREE

Maggie strode quickly down the hallway leading to the kitchen, resolute and determined. Just before reaching the kitchen door, she suddenly stopped, leaned against the wall, and listened to the jovial comradery of those inside. *My family*, she smiled, but then frowned. *No, Alfred is my family, my love. These are only temporary . . . until I am reunited with my one true love.*

A momentary sense of guilt flowed over her as she stepped around the corner and was met with exuberance and welcome.

"Maggie! You're here," grinned Sarah. "We're so glad to see you. Dad wouldn't let us eat until you got here. I think," she whispered loudly, "he has a crush on you." She giggled, but then stopped at the curious confusion on Maggie's face.

"What? He wishes to crush me?" Unbidden tears filled her eyes, and she prepared to leave.

"Oh, no, Maggie dear." Magdalyn quickly placed her arm around Maggie's shoulder. "Sarah didn't mean that

Hatchet wanted to harm you, but that he likes you . . . a lot. As we all do," she hastened to add.

"But not as much as Dad does," Sarah giggled.

Maggie glanced quickly at Hatchet, as he turned away in embarrassment, her own cheeks slightly pinked. "Oh." She said softly, sudden guilt filling her heart as what she was about to do. *But it has to be. If not now, I will never have the courage to return to my . . . one . . . true . . . love.*

She smiled brightly, and said, "I see he is hard at work, but I have a surprise for you. We will not be having lunch here, at home."

"We won't?" chorused the three. "But—"

"No, my darlings." She took a deep breath and turned to Hatchet. "Hatchet . . . um . . . do you remember the hidden stream, down by the waterfall, I took you to once?"

"Y-y-y-yes, Ma'am. Right purty place it is being, that it is."

"Well, my darlings, I thought it would make a lovely change of pace if we had our noon meal, somewhere outside of this cavern. Somewhere lovely and serene. We could make a day of it. We have all worked so hard, a change of pace would be in order, don't you think?"

"Oh, Maggie, what a super idea. I'd love to see the waterfall, wouldn't you Dad?"

"As she said, Oi've been there, and I be thinkin' it be the perfect place to be spending the day." He turned toward Magdalyn. "An w'at do you be thinkin', yer ladyship?"

Magdalyn stared at the happy troop, and said, "It sounds like a wonderful idea. Is it far? How long will it take us to get there?"

"That depends," Maggie smiled. "If we choose to walk, perhaps by morning. However, if you don't mind flying, we could be there within the hour. Of, course, I would need to take a couple of trips, as I don't think I could handle three people all at the same time. Perhaps I could take Will, I mean Hatchet, and the food, first, so that he can prepare our meal, and then return for Magdalyn and Sarah. If that would be agreeable to all, that is."

Hatchet grinned and started packing food and supplies, while Magdalyn and Sarah began packing up plates, cups and tableware, such as it was.

"Excellent!" Maggie exclaimed. "We shall begin forthwith. Oh, please excuse me. I have to take care of one little item first. It will be a long, but happy and productive day, I am certain. I shall return momentarily. Hopefully everything will be ready by then. Anyone else need to take care of . . . um . . . anything before we go? No? Good, I will be right back "

As preparations were being made in the kitchen, Maggie hurried to her room and grabbed two small bottles, one she quickly opened, and daubed a small amount of the precious liquid on her throat and on both wrists. After all, a lady must always smell lovely, for the man in her life. Tucking both bottles into a small satchel, she hurried back to the kitchen. Grabbing a large leather pouch, she threw in several pieces of firewood, and left it at the entrance while she went to retrieve Hatchet and the necessary items for their lunch in the woods.

A short time later, Hatchet had the fire going and was preparing their meal. Maggie took to the air and was soon back at the cavern where Magdalyn and Sarah patiently waited. In no time at all, it seemed, Maggie landed at the forest clearing, and the four were seated around a lovely campfire eating the lunch Hatchet had so painstakingly prepared.

"That was wonderful," sighed Magdalyn, as Sarah was chasing a fish, with her hand, in the stream. "We should try this again someday . . . if it is alright with you, of course, Maggie dear. You have outdone yourself. And Hatchet, you are to be commended as well. A wonderful lunch at such a beautiful place. I'm almost sad that it will soon be over."

"Not so soon," smiled Maggie. "I have brought a

surprise for all of you." She reached into another satchel and pulled out a scrumptious looking chocolate pudding. "Here we go. I have prepared enough for all. It's my own recipe, you see. I hope you like it."

"It looks super, Maggie," gushed Sarah. "I can't wait to try it."

"Then don't. Why wait? It is to be enjoyed now." She smiled sweetly. The three practically inhaled the pudding when Sarah stopped and asked," But what about you, Maggie. This is the best pudding I have ever had. Aren't you going to have . . . some?"

"Later, child . . . later." She watched as first Sarah, and then Magdalyn and finally Hatchet closed their eyes in sleep.

"W'at 'ave . . . ye . . . done, ye . . . black . . . demon?" whimpered Hatchet as his head slipped to one side and he was soon curled up on the ground, snoring loudly.

"Only what I had to do, Hatchet." She crept over to the sleeping Magdalyn and brushed the hair from her forehead. "I'm so sorry, Magdalyn. I have learned to really like you. You are truly worthy, but I must know for certain whether Alfred loves me as much as he does you. You see, he is my life, and I fear I cannot live without him. Please understand, it is the only way."

She uncorked a third vial and downed its contents. A blinding flash of light, and the black dragon disappeared. In its place a replica of Alfred's beloved Magdalyn now stood. "You see, Magdalyn, he will not even know the difference. I will be you, and no one will be able to tell the real me. In this way I can find out his true feelings, and if he still loves you more than me, I will return leaving him unharmed. However, if he truly does love me best, we shall see what we shall see. Sweet dreams, my darlings. We shall not meet again until it is over. Good night, and farewell."

After casting a quick spell of protection over the sleeping trio, Maggie disappeared, reappearing at the entrance to the cavern. There was no time like the present to implement her plan. No time like the present.

CHAPTER TWENTY-FOUR

Maggie hurried into the laboratory, and glancing quickly about the room, called out, "Rocky? . . . Rocky, where are you? I need you."

"I am right here, Madam. On the shelf, where I sadly must always stay, cooped up in this lonely room with nowhere to go and nothing to do. No one to talk to. My life is so dismal. It's nice of you to come by, once in a while, to ease my loneliness." He sighed deeply.

"Well, um, yes. I do what I can. But I need you to contact Max and tell him I need to speak to Alfred . . . my beloved, as soon as possible. And hurry. I must speak to him post haste."

Alfred? . . . Post haste? Hmmm. "As you wish, Madam. Perhaps you would wish to take a short respite while I make the call. It may take a while."

"I don't have time for a respite. I need to speak to my beloved now."

"As you wish, Madam. I will do my best, but these things take time. I really think it would be in your best interest to—"

"Did I ask you? Well then, do as I ask. I will wait." She began to pace the laboratory, from one end to the next.

"Beg pardon, Madam, but is everything all right? You seem a bit agitated."

"How I am feeling is none of your concern. However, I will be much improved if you stop talking and get me my *husband*."

"As you wish, Madam," Rocky replied icily. "As you wish."

"Yes, as I wish, and I do wish it now."

Rocky thought of a quick retort but dismissed it as soon as it came to mind. Madam was clearly not in the best frame of mind, and if he could make it even a little better, he would certainly try. "Rocky to Max . . . Rocky to Max . . . Come in please . . . ."

Over and over he repeated the words until Maggie thought she would certainly go mad. *Time . . . time . . . not much time . . . .*

"I am sorry Madam, but it appears Max is occupied elsewhere. I will keep trying but are you certain you do not wish a short rest while this is going on. It could take some time, you know. He could be having a bit of revelry with the boy, you see."

Maggie glared at the golem, then softened. "I do seem to be a bit overwrought; I think I will take a quick rest while you are trying your best to reach my beloved." She smiled at the golem. "You *will* let me know as soon as you have reached him, will you not?"

"Of course, Madam. Will you be leaving us shortly? Is that why you are in such a hurry. I don't blame you, if you are. I would love to travel, to see the world. You are so fortunate to live in the outside world. Not trapped in this prison . . . forever, and ever, and ever." He groaned with excessive volume. "I—"

"Rocky, just call!" she snapped. "I mean, I would appreciate it if you would tend to these matters as soon as possible. I will be in my room when you need me." She smiled sweetly and hurried out of the laboratory. "Thank you, Rocky," she called as she left the room. *That golem needs to be replace*d, she grunted as she rushed down the hall to her suite. A little rest would do her good. After all, she did want to look her best when she saw Alfred again. She smiled softly at the thought, before reclining on her cot and closing her eyes.

***

Madam, wake up, I have Max on the line. Please wake up and answer his call. You don't want to miss it. *Hmmm. No answer. Perhaps she has retired to another room, or perhaps she has left the premises. I shall call louder.* MADAM! DO YOU HEAR ME? MAX IS ON THE LINE, WITH YOUR DEARLY BELOVED. COME QUICKLY TO THE LABORATORY, OR YOU MAY MSS HIS CALL! *There, that should do it.* Rocky grinned to himself. *I've always wanted to do that. Now to wait and see if it worked.*

"Wha'." Maggie jumped from her cot and stared blearily around her room. *Rocky? Max? Master? Um . . . Alfred? "Oh."*

As quickly as she could muster, she threw on a housecoat and raced to the laboratory. Bursting through the door, she panted, "Have you reached him? Have you reached my beloved?"

She grabbed the golem and breathlessly cried, "Master? I mean, Alfred? Is it you, my love?" She cringed at her faux pas and waited anxiously for the sound of his voice.

"Magdalyn, is that you? Since when do you call me master?"

"Oh, my love, it's so good to hear your voice at last. I have missed you so."

"I have missed you desperately as well. But I'm confused. What is this master thing?"

"Oh, my darling. Please forgive me. I have been so long

a prisoner of that, that dragon, I have gotten used to hearing you addressed as such, but not anymore. I'm coming home, but I need your help in getting back into the great room . . . the, um, sealing spell and all, you know."

"You have no idea how wonderful it is to hear your voice. I have been driving everyone crazy with worry. How did you escape? Is Sarah with you? When can you get here? I will be waiting with bells on . . . so to speak. I will have Merlin present to unlock the painting, but it will need to be resealed once you get here . . . for everyone's safety, you know. We don't want Maggie following you in, and we all know she will certainly try."

"Would that be so bad, my love, to see her again?"

"It could very well be a tragedy for all of us, if you know what I mean."

"Y-yes, of course. But perhaps she has changed for the better."

"You don't know her like I do. She will never change, and the best thing we can do is to keep her out of our lives, forever."

Maggie swallowed back the tears and quickly changed the subject. "I can be there in an hour, but I cannot bring Sarah with me. It seems she has been bewitched by, um, that black-hearted dragon and chose not to come with me. Oh,

Alfred, I need to see you as soon as possible. I should go. The sooner I leave, the sooner I can be back in your arms where I belong."

"I will see you in one hour. I will find Merlin and drag him here, if I have to. Until then, my love. Hurry back to me. I'll be waiting not-so-patiently for your return." He placed the golem back on his perch, patted him briefly on his stone head, and ran through the great room door joyfully screaming, "She's coming home. She's coming home. Merlin, where are you? She's coming home."

CHAPTER TWENTY-FIVE

Magdalyn stirred. Someone was gently shaking her. It was still dark. Why was someone disturbing her sleep? It's not time to get up, yet. She slapped at the air. "Go back to bed. It's not yet light. I'm so tired. Sleep , , , sleep . . . wonderful . . . sleep?" She awoke with a start. "Sarah? Hatchet? Where are we? What's going on?"

"Tha' black demon spelled us to sleep, she did. I'm afeared she cud uv took on yer ladyship's form an' left us 'ere, to try to trick th' marster into believin' she was you. No gud will come o' that."

"What? We have to get back to the caves. Perhaps we can stop her before she does something we may all regret."

"Beg pardon, ma'am, but the she devil has been gone fer hours. These woods be treacherous, 'specially in the dark. There be no way we can be leavin' before dawn. Sorry, yer ladyship. But she be trickin' us all. We'll be leavin' first thing in the morn."

"But we can't wait until morning. We need to leave now."

"It's bein' too dangerous to travel at night in these woods. We jest hav' t' wait 'til morn and do the best we kin . . . O'I mean can."

"Dad's right, Magdalyn. If we tried to leave tonight, we could be eaten, or something. And besides, Alfred isn't stupid. He'll see right through her, I'm sure. She won't be able to fool him, and then, then . . . I'll feel sorry for her. She won't get away with this, I promise."

"My darling girl," Magdalyn sighed. "I appreciate your sentiments, but you are just a child. She is a determined dragon in a woman's body. And how can a man resist one so determined, she would steal another woman's features? All we can do now is pray that he will see through her trickery, and not succumb to her wiles. It appears there is enough to eat for supper, so I say we eat, retire, get up early and leave for home at first light."

"As you say, yer ladyship. But it be a long walk back to camp, and hurry as we will, we may not be there until tomorrow eve."

The woman does not yet realize I have a few tricks up my own sleeve. Watch out Maggie. We are coming for you, ready or not.

* * *

Maggie stood in the pathway, just outside the painting

portal, and paced in place. *Where are they? I don't know how long I can stay in this disguise. I feel like I am weakening. Hurry, Alfred. I will do much better when I see you and you hold me in your arms.*

At that moment, the great room door burst open and Alfred flew in, followed closely by Merlin, Bee and Gwenny.

"May the saints be praised," Gwenny shrieked as she ran toward the painting. "You're here at last."

"Hurry, Merlin. Speed it up a bit will you. I can hardly believe it, she's back."

"I'm working as fast as I can. If you will let go of me, I can probably work a lot faster."

Maggie watched nervously while Merlin attempted to untangle himself from Alfred's grip, glanced quickly behind her as if the evil dragon herself, was at her heels, then turned back to Alfred, love flowing from her eyes and her smile.

Oh, Master . . . um, Alfred, I am so glad to have found you at last. I knew I would, if I kept trying hard enough. She doesn't deserve you, my love, but I will love you forever.

She flinched, just a bit, and her smile faded momentarily at the thought of Hatchet, and those left behind – her family. *No!* she argued with herself, *Alfred is my family! Only Alfred.* She quickly brightened, her smile returning with the love she had for Alfred. *But . . . Hatchet?*

He really isn't the idiot I once thought him, and he does kind of grow on you. She smiled inside, then frowned. *No, no, no. I can't worry about him now. I am about to be reunited with my one true love.* She smiled once again, ignoring the niggling at the back of her brain.

At last the seal was broken and Maggie flew into the arms of her beloved. "Oh, um, Alfred, I have missed you so."

Alfred wrapped his arms around his 'wife' and hugged her fiercely. "You must never return to this room again," he whispered. "I could not bear it, if I lost you again."

"Do not worry, my love. I will never leave you again. Never." She snuggled deeper into her 'husband's' arms and was content. The family rejoiced, for Magdalyn was back where she belonged.

* * *

"This is getting us nowhere. Do you have any idea, any idea at all, where we are?" Magdalyn sighed and dropped onto a mossy hill, her head in her hands, her soul slipping into despair.

"O'i know not these woods, yer ladyship. O'i 'ave hunted over most of this cursed island, but never 'ave o'i seen this place."

"Dad," interrupted Sarah. "You're regressing in your speech. You were doing so well, but you're slipping back into your old way of talking. Magdalyn might not understand you, like I do."

"I understood every word, but if we are going to make it out of these woods we are going to have to work together. And Hatchet, dear, it really would be best if you could try to speak more clearly. When we get back to civilization, you will command more respect from your peers, if you do. So, it's for your benefit, more than ours. Do you understand, sir?"

"Oi'm not stupid, ye know," he growled testily.

"I never thought you were. In fact, the very opposite, I would say. Intelligence reeks from you, so that is why I think it would be in your best interest to show that intelligence to those around you. Yes? Set them all straight." She grinned at the outlaw. "Show them what you're made of." She smacked her left hand with her right fist to add emphasis to her words.

"Yes, ma'am!" Hatchet grinned, in spite of himself, straightening his shoulders, and lifting his head high. "O'I, I mean, *I* can do this."

"Hatchet, dear. Do you think you could climb this tree, and find out where we are, and how far it is to the forest end, and in which direction we need to go? I have an idea, but I need to know where we are first."

"At yer service, yer ladyship, I mean Magdalyn, ma'am." He briefly saluted and then began to climb.

"What's your idea, Magdalyn?" Sarah asked. "We can't exactly fly out of here."

"True, but we might be able to ride in style. Help me gather some vines and limbs, will you, dear?"

"Uh, sure. But what are we going to do with them?"

"We are going to make a sleigh, of sorts."

"What for? We don't have anything to pull it."

Magdalyn smiled. "Don't worry, dear. Something will probably come up. Have faith."

Sarah didn't have a lot of faith, but she did what she was asked anyway. Before long, Hatchet had shimmied down the tree, and stood dejectedly before them.

"It be straight ahead, as the crow flies, so tha' part be gud. We be goin' the right direction, but it be at least 5 mile to th' border. "Even if we get t' the meadow, it be still a far piece t' home. We'll never make it in toime."

"Of, course, we will." Magdalyn smiled broadly. "Sarah and I have made suitable transportation. Please sit down and grab a vine."

Hatchet stared at the makeshift sleigh, and then at

Sarah. "Bonkers she is. A bit daft," he whispered in Sarah's ear. "This all mus' be a bit too much fer her ladyship. "

"You know, Hatchet, I have exceptional hearing. I am not daft, but I do suggest you hang on tight." Placing two fingers against the sides of her mouth, she whistled long and shrill. From out of the woods, stepped two beautiful, sleek, but very large elk, walking straight to Magdalyn and nuzzling her as if she were a dear friend.

Whispering something into their ears, she quickly took the makeshift harness, and fastened it as securely around the elk as she could. "There," she turned to the others, "are we ready to go?" She stepped carefully onto the sleigh and settled in. "All right, boys, let's go home."

Hatchet turned to Sarah, his mouth agape. Sarah simply shrugged and gripped her vine even tighter. Her eyes flew open as the elk began to walk, and then run, as swift as the wind, straight and true. Sarah grinned, holding the vine with one hand, the other gripping the arm of her shrieking 'dad'.

"This is so cool," she shouted. She leaned toward Magdalyn. "I knew you could come up with something, but this is even cooler than cool."

"Thank you, my darling girl. We'll be home before you can say—" But her words were lost as the elk took to the sky, and they were soon soaring over the tree-tops.

Hatchet squeezed his eyes shut as tightly as he could, and held all the tighter to his vines, but Sarah enjoyed every minute of this unexpected journey.

CHAPTER TWENTY-SIX

Maggie stared at the quantity of makeup products on the dressing table and wondered what to do next. *No wonder Magdalyn is so beautiful, with all these beauty things to use. But how does she do it. What should I do first? I can be beautiful, too. I just need to learn what to do.* She ignored the persistent tugging at her sleeve.

"Gwamma. Gwamma!" Amanda Joy was getting frustrated. Her grandmother had always been available to talk to her, to hold her, to pay attention to her. But now . . . . Something was wrong. But what? She looked like Gwamma, but she didn't act like Gwamma.

Finally, Maggie noticed the little girl, and turned to stare pointedly at her. "What do you want, child? Can't you see I'm busy?"

The little girl's eyes filled with tears, and she spoke low and slow. "You not my gwamma. My gwamma nice, and she wuvs me. And she know my name. She never call me what you did. I gonna tell." She ran toward the door.

"Come back," Maggie Panicked. "I didn't mean—"

But Amanda Joy was gone.

Maggie stopped what she was doing and raced after the little girl, grabbing her just before she reached the middle of hallway. She placed her hand over the child's mouth and received a nasty bite for her efforts. Amanda Joy shrieked as she was dropped, before whipping around, and glaring at her 'grandmother.'

"What is going on here?" bellowed Alfred as he ran into the hall and pulled the tot into his arms.

"The little witch bit me, I mean the child bit me." She covered her hand and smiled sweetly. "Unfortunately, we had a misunderstanding and she got a little upset. It meant nothing, really."

Alfred was confused. Shifting Amanda Joy in his arms, he asked, "Amanda, dear, what happened? Why are you mad at Grandma?"

"That not gwamma," she bristled, her tiny arms across her chest.

"Of course, she is, sweetheart. Doesn't she look and sound just like Grandma? It's just been awhile since you've seen her. Tell Grandma you're sorry for hurting her."

"Not sorry. She not my gwamma. She not know my name, and she mean to me." Tears filled her eyes.

Alfred was beginning to become a bit concerned. "How

so, little one?" He smiled apologetically at 'Magdalyn.'

"I'm sure Grandma loves you a whole bunch."

"No, she doesn't!" scowled Amanda Joy. "Make her go way."

"But Amanda, she just got back," comforted Alfred. "You don't want her to leave already, do you?"

"Yes! I want my real gwamma back."

Exasperated, Alfred put his granddaughter back on the floor and patted her backside. "Why don't you run out back and talk to Sure-shot while I have a talk with, um, Grandma."

"That—not—my—gwamma!" Amanda Joy growled but ran outside to find her brother anyway. Maybe he could help.

Alfred took 'Magdalyn' into his arms. "I'm so sorry, my love," he soothed. "What happened in there? She seemed so happy to have you back, as are we all."

"Unfortunately, I was distracted, and didn't notice her at first, when she was trying to get my attention, and I called her child instead of Amanda, and she freaked out. I guess I *have* been away too long. But I'm back now, and hopefully I'll be able to become my old self again, rather quickly, and do what I must to regain peace, and the love of my family."

"Magdalyn, you are back, and you are safe among those

who love you more than life itself."

Maggie snuggled in a little closer. "Do you really love me, Ma-Alfred? As much as I love you?"

"Magdalyn, my love. You are the only woman I have ever loved. There has never been another as precious as you."

Maggie's eyes filled with tears, and she stiffened slightly. "Not even Maggie, that, that black dragon? You told me you loved her, too."

"And that was true, at one time. She was all I had, and I thought I would never see you again. But my love, or should I say, infatuation, with Maggie was more as a . . . I don't know. But certainly, you don't think I could love a dragon more than you. You are my life, the mother of my child, the grandmother of my grandchildren. My first, my only true love."

"I understand," murmured Maggie, her heart broken. She now knew what she had come to find out, and it was almost more than she could bear. "Excuse me, my love, but I think I had best lay down for a bit. This whole episode has exhausted me."

"Of, course, my dear. Go and get some rest. As you know, Gwenny has something scrumptious planned for tonight, as usual. I'll come and get you when it's time. Feel better, and I'll see you in an hour or so." Alfred watched her as she lumbered toward the bedroom. *Something is wrong. I can feel it. But what? Something just doesn't feel right about this whole thing. And why this sudden interest in Maggie? Twice now, she started to call me . . . Master, was it? That is not like Magdalyn. Maggie, perhaps, but . . . never . . . Magdalyn. Something is very, very wrong.*

* * *

Maggie gathered her few personal belongings, tears of anger and frustration blurring her vision. *So, Magdalyn is your only love, is she? Did you ever really love **me**, or was I just a temporary plaything, until you could return to your 'one true love?'*

She quickly recovered, cautiously opened her bedroom door and peeked into the hallway. *Clear.* Silently creeping down the hall, she found her way to the great room. She was going home. *There are people on the island who truly love me, even if Alfred does not. I have my family, and I will keep them . . . every one of them. I will go to the meadow and bring my real family home. Alfred can just suffer . . . just like I am suffering.* She smiled grimly and opened the great room door.

* * *

"It's been hours," whined Sarah. "When are we going to get

there? There's no telling what damage Maggie might have already done. When are we going to get back to the cave?"

"Sarah, dear. I, too, would like to get back as soon as possible, but like us, these animals have run for hours. They're tired and doing their best to get us where we need to go in the most expedient manner. Let's all have some patience, okay?"

"Patience be . . . um, beg pardon yer ladyship, uh, Magdalyn. Look! The cavern be in sight. Not one hour left, 'til we get there."

"Really? Yea!" Sarah whooped.

"And sooner than that, according to the elk," Magdalyn grinned. "I think they sense, we're almost home. Hang on tight, everybody. We're picking up speed."

Sarah gasped as the elk seemed to fly across the island plain. Hanging on tightly to her rope with one hand, and Hatchet with the other, she shrieked with delight. In no time at all, it seemed, the elk slowed to a walk, and stopped soon after that at the opening to the cave, panting as if they would never get a decent breath again. But they were at their destination, so that was really all that mattered, wasn't it?

"Everybody out," Magdalyn ordered as she quickly unhitched the elk. Handing the make-shift reins to Hatchet she said, "Hatchet, dear, would you mind taking the elk to the pasture and giving them some food and water. They must be exhausted, as well as hungry and thirsty, after running, as they did, all this way."

"It would be my pleasure, yer ladyship, uh, Magdalyn, ma'am. But cud ye do me a favor and call me Will. That be me given name, and oi, um, I would be tha' honored if ye cud call me by the name me mother gived me."

"Will . . . What a lovely name . . . a strong name. Just like the man who holds the name. It would be my pleasure, Will."

Hatchet beamed and took the reins from Magdalyn. "Ye had best hurry to the laboratory, Magdalyn, ma'am. Tell Rocky to call Max and let him know yer alright." With shoulders as straight as he could get them, he led the elk to the pasture, and their much-needed care. "Will," he murmured. "That's moi, um *my* name, and a roight gud one at that." He grinned to himself and then disappeared into the former dragon nesting cavern. *Will . . .*

"Wow, Magdalyn. You're the only one he has ever let call him Will. You, yer ladyship," she giggled, "certainly have a way with people."

"Well," Magdalyn cocked her head. "It is as it should be and should always have been. You can't expect someone to feel respected, unless they know they are respected."

"I know, but you do it so well. I'm proud of you, and I'm proud of Dad, too."

"As you should be. Now, young lady, let's get to the laboratory before it *is* too late."

* * *

Maggie slumped in front of the painting of the dark forest and stared at the pathway where she had so recently stood, wishing she had never come. Alfred didn't love her . . . at least not like she wanted to be loved. It was Magdalyn all along. *Magdalyn. Magdalyn!* She wanted to scream but knew that it wasn't really Magdalyn's fault Alfred loved her so much.

Magdalyn wasn't what she first thought. She was a true lady. *But I can be a lady, too. If given half a chance. But no one is willing to give me that chance.* She scowled, then smiled softly. *Except for my family – Hatchet, Sarah, and Magdalyn, the lady herself, and a dear friend. I must go back and make it right somehow. But can they ever forgive me for what I've done?* Tears began to freely flow, as she buried her face in her hands.

"Magdalyn? Magdalyn, my dear. Whatever is the matter? Bee, followed closely by Gwenny, slipped quietly into the great room and moved quickly to 'Magdalyn's' side. "Magdalyn? Are you alright?"

Maggie stiffened, but did not turn around. "I have done some terrible things," she whispered. "I should not be here. I am going back to the island where I belong. Good-bye. And tell the child I didn't mean to upset her. I guess I was just not thinking straight. And tell Alfred . . . tell him I love him, but not enough to stay. Again, I say . . . good-bye."

She walked straight ahead and into the painting. She stood on the pathway, for just a moment, turned, and reached her hand toward the great room. *Good, it is still sealed from this side. There is no going back. I must go home where I belong . . . with those who love me for who I am – my family.* She turned around and walked into the woods. As soon as she was out of sight, she morphed back into the dragon and began the long trek back to the island. *I'm coming, my family. I'm coming home.*

Bee turned to Gwenny. "What just happened?" she asked, as Alfred, Merlin and Sure-shot burst into the room. But it was too late. 'Magdalyn' was gone.

.

CHAPTER TWENTY-SEVEN

"Madam," Rocky startled. "How did you return so quickly? Was your husband not happy to see you?"

Sarah stared at the golem. "What are you talking about, Rocky. We only just got here. Maggie took us far away and abandoned us. We got back as quick as we could."

"But I don't understand." He turned toward Magdalyn. "She said she was you. She looked like you and sounded like you. Was it not you who stood before me, and used me to talk to my old master, Alfred? But, if it was not you, my lady, then . . . then . . . oh woe is me. She tricked me. She tricked me and went in your place.

"Oh, help. I have been shamefully tricked. But, are you certain you are not she, the one who apparently tricked me into believing she was you so that I would help her reunite with her husband who . . . wasn't really . . . her . . . husband? Oh, dear, you might as well melt me where I stand. Dump me in that bucket of water by the sink. I don't deserve to live. I cannot go on in this agony. Oh, woe is me. I am undone. Tricked . . . by the evil one. I cannot bear to live with this shame. Destroy me, for I am not worth existing."

"Is he always like this?" asked Magdalyn.

"Sometimes even worse."

"Okay, Rocky," Magdalyn soothed, "snap out of it. We don't blame you for anything. Maggie can be quite persuasive when she wants to be."

"But I should have known. I suspected, but she was so convincing . . . as you, my lady . . . of course. I know I did terribly wrong. You have every right to discipline me . . . to destroy me, even." He began to sob.

"Rocky, dear. Please don't cry. We know it was not your fault, and if you cry you will melt, and if you melt you will be no good for anyone. Now, dry those tears, and tell us exactly what happened.

Reluctantly, Rocky dried his tears and began his tale of woe.

* * *

"What just happened?!" bellowed Alfred. "Where did she go, and why did you let her leave?"

"Will someone please tell me what has happened here." Merlin strode toward the painting, peering intently into the darkness. "Maggie." Was all he said.

"I knew it! And so did Amanda Joy. She said that woman was not her grandmother. I just didn't want to believe it. I desired my wife back so desperately, I *wanted* to believe her. I *needed* to believe her. But it was Maggie all the time. I should have known." He turned toward Merlin. "What are we going to do? If she has hurt Magdalyn in any way, I will destroy her."

"Now, let's not jump to any conclusions. First, we need to go back to the island. We will find her and make her give Magdalyn and Sarah back to us."

"And how do you suppose we do that? The island is very large and there are a million hiding places. I should know, I lived there long enough." Alfred muttered.

"Alfred? I'm with Merlin," Bee broke in. "Apparently, or obviously, it was Maggie, but she seemed so upset, so sorry for what she said she'd done. Maybe we should find out the circumstances before we jump to too many conclusions."

"Nonsense!" snapped Alfred. "Maggie is evil and cannot be trusted. We need to find and destroy her before she does any more damage."

"We will find her, and we will get Magdalyn and Sarah back, but we need to do it with a cool head, not just jump into the middle of things without thinking."

"I *have* been thinking, and thinking, and thinking. Ever since she stole my life from me, I've been thinking. And she will not get away with it any longer."

"Well, then," Merlin cleared his throat. "Perhaps we should begin our search. But," he admonished Alfred, "only with a cool head, and not out of anger, or revenge. Do we all understand?"

Everyone nodded but Alfred.

"Alfred?" Bee placed a hand on his forearm. "Alfred, it's important that we do this the right way. Are you with us, or against us?"

"I'll do anything to get my wife back," he muttered. "But if she has harmed one hair on my beloved's head, I can't promise anything."

"Fine, but if she has not harmed her, don't do anything you shouldn't do. Promise?"

"I promise nothing, but I will do the best I can, and that will have to be enough."

"Noted," smiled Bee. "And I am certain you will do the right thing when the time comes."

"I'll go get Dad, and the rest of the family. We're going to need all the help we can get." Sure-shot ran from the great room, determined to find, and recruit, all interested rescuers as soon as possible. Time was of the essence.

* * *

Maggie stood at the laboratory door and watched 'her

family' attempt to console the little golem. She couldn't hear what they were saying, but it was obvious something was not quite right. The golem knew the hazards of moisture, but yet he was sobbing . . . as if he wished to die. *Enough . . . this has got to stop now.*

"What is going on here?" Maggie demanded. "Is the whole world going mad?"

"Maggie!" cried Sarah. "You *are* here. You didn't leave us after all . . . . did you?"

"Unfortunately, I did. But I have learned my lesson, and it was a costly one. And you," she pointed to Magdalyn, "lied to me."

"What? What are you talking about?' asked Sarah. "You're the one who left us miles and miles away from anything. Thanks to Magdalyn, we were able to make it home safely. You would have left us there to die."

"Never, my child. I knew you would find your way home." she stared pointedly at Magdalyn. "I just didn't know how quickly. Had you not been here when I returned, I would have found you and brought you home myself. But it seems it was not necessary. "

"I warned you, Maggie, I was not as helpless as you might like to think I was. But it's good to see you have returned anyway. How was your excursion?" Magdalyn smiled sweetly, but knowingly.

"You lied to me. Why did you lie? Just so my heart would be broken all over again? You hate me, don't you."

"Maggie, dear, I have no idea what you ae talking about. And we don't hate you. You are our friend . . . our benefactor."

But Maggie was without understanding as she snapped, "You told me Alfred loved me, but it was all a lie. All he loves is you . . . traitor."

"Maggie, dear. Of course, he loves you. I tried to tell you earlier. He has enough love for both of us, but in different ways. Me, as his wife, you, as his best dragon friend. Do you understand, now? Please, Maggie, don't cry. Remember, we are family – you, Sarah, Will and myself. We may not always show our love to each other, but it's there. We just need to show it more often, I suppose. But running off and leaving us behind was not a very good way to show *you* cared, was it, dear one."

Maggie stared at her family, and once again tears started to flow. She didn't see Hatchet as he silently entered the laboratory, and stood behind her, just listening. "How can you be so nice to me, after . . . ." she sniffed, and then began to wail. "I did what I had to do . . . and lost. I am fearfully ashamed, and sorrowful for my misdeeds. Can you

all forgive me . . . my family?" She tried to smile through
her tears but was barely successful.

"There's nothing to be ashamed of," soothed Magdalyn.
"Yes, what you did was not exactly family-like, but you
were a woman in love. I, too, am a woman in love, so I
cannot fault you your feelings. But we are family, and we
will stick together, through thick or thin. We will make it
through this." She put her arms around Maggie, joined by,
first Sarah, and then Hatchet. Together they stood, for quite
some time, letting lose the pain and the shame of what had
been done.

"I must take you back," Maggie sniffed once again.
"Back where you belong. But I will stay here . . . where I
belong. Ellie was right. I am not suited to rule. I am too
selfish, and blind and . . . too much like Chi – a warrior
through and through."

"But Maggie, that can be a good thing," Sarah broke in.
"Every country needs its warriors, its soldiers, to be safe,
and protect all the citizens. Even though I think you would
make a great queen, maybe it's your destiny to protect rather
than to rule."

"Chi? Lark's Chi?" Magdalyn was awed. "Why didn't
you tell me?" She clapped her hands. "Oh, how wonderful.
You must tell me all about it."

"But I need to take you home. Alfred wants you to come home, as does the rest of your family. You need to be with family."

"But we are with family, Maggie. Just another branch. Look, Maggie, dear. I would like to go home and see my husband, and the rest of the family more than anything in the world. But it is late, and we still need to talk. Tomorrow will be soon enough. What do you say we all have something to eat, have a good long talk, and go home first thing in the morning? Yes? Good. Now, tell me about Chi."

* * *

I am sorry, Master. It appears that Rocky has tried to contact us, but has been unsuccessful."

"What do you mean, he's been unsuccessful? Can he no longer communicate?"

"I am not certain, Master. It sounded like he had been . . . crying? He knows better than that. He could melt away to nothing. Oh, woe is me. Am I going to lose my brother as well?"

Max. Don't you start crying. We don't want to lose both of you." Bee soothed.

"Lose? Both of us? Oh, dear. We are doomed."

"Not yet, we're not." Alfred glared into space. "Like it, or not, we are going to the island, first thing in the morning.

And then she will pay," he muttered. "She will surely pay for the harm she has done. This, I swear."

CHAPTER TWENTY-EIGHT

"Well, my dear ones. Are you ready to go home . . . to your other home, I mean?" Maggie smiled affectionately at her 'family' and they smiled back.

"Sure thing," Sarah gushed, "but we have dibs on coming back to see you really soon. Okay?"

"Absolutely, my darling daughter. The sooner the better. But . . . say, have you been growing while you have been here? You look like you might be at least a head taller than when you first came."

"I think she's right, Sarah, dear." Magdalyn stood with her arms crossed and stared at the not-so-little girl. "I'd swear you were almost as tall as me, now. And perhaps a bit heavier, as well. That may pose a problem for Maggie. She is very strong and powerful, but I think we've all put on a little weight during the past few weeks," she raised an eyebrow and grinned at Hatchet. "No offence, dear Will."

"None taken, yer ladyship . . . um . . . Magdalyn, ma'am."

Maggie smiled. She truly loved this 'family' and hated

the thought of missing them so much, but they had promised to visit very soon, so she was content. *All is as it should be, no matter how painful it has become, to part.* "Ha-hum," she cleared her throat, just a bit gravelly. "This talk is all lovely, but I think we had best be on our way, before I cannot stand to let you depart." She sighed dramatically, then grinned again. "However, I do think Magdalyn, my dear sister, has a point. Sarah is simply growing up, and Hatchet has just been subject to good cooking. Under the circumstances, I do think it would be best if we did this transfer in installments.

"I will take Sarah and Magdalyn on this first trip, then come back and get you, Hatchet. If that's alright with you." She spoke to the group, but her question was aimed at Hatchet.

"Tha' will be fine, Maggie. Jest don' be away too long. I be missing ye already." He flushed and hastened to add. "All of ye oi, uh, *I* mean."

"Of, course, you do. We all understand, don't we, Maggie . . . Sarah." Magdalyn smiled.

"I do," Sarah reached out and hugged her 'dad'. "I will always love you, and I'll miss you more than you will ever know. And you, too, Maggie. You are the best dragon friend I have ever had . . . AND you are very beautiful whether as a dragon or a lady."

"Do you really think so?"

"Absolutely," broke in Magdalyn. "You are beautiful both inside and out. However, if we are going to make it back to the dark woods, in time, we had best hurry. I don't want Alfred to do something rash, and perhaps destroy everything we have worked so hard for."

Maggie frowned. "You are right, as usual, Magdalyn. Even though it pains me deeply, I can no longer forestall the inevitable. Come, climb aboard and we shall be on our way. I am going to miss you so much."

Sarah wrapped her arms around Maggie's neck and hugged her fiercely. "Me, too, Maggie. And don't forget, you are loved, and we will see you again very, very soon." She scampered up Maggie's wing and settled behind Magdalyn, wrapping her arms securely around her waist. "Okay, I'm ready." She turned to Hatchet. "I love you, Dad. We'll see you soon."

Maggie sniffed, spread her wings and took to the sky.

Hatchet's face was solemn as he fought back the tears. He was a strong man, and really shouldn't be seen as an emotional wreck, but he couldn't stop a tiny tear from slipping down his weathered cheek. "Oi'll see you soon . . . dautter. I . . . love ye . . . too." *All of ye*. And they were gone.

* * *

Alfred was up before dawn, pacing the carpet in front of the locked painting. For some crazy reason he could not enter the painting, no matter how hard he tried. And he had tried, for hours, it seemed. The door slid open and Merlin swept through - Gwenny, Bee, and the family close behind. The only one noticeably missing was Robert. For some reason, he felt it necessary to seek out Ellie, and thus his presence was missed.

"Ah, Alfred, my friend. We thought we might find you here. You missed a marvelous breakfast. Our Gwenny, here, is the best, at breakfast . . . or lunch . . . or dinner." He patted his overfull stomach. "Quite a woman we have here."

"Quite a woman *you* have, you mean." Alfred snapped, but then softened. "My apologies, Gwenny." Then hardened again. "Mine is at the mercy of the epitome of evil."

"Now, Alfred, you don't know that. Magdalyn could have her eating out of her hand, as far as we know." Bee soothed.

"*You* don't know Maggie like I do. She would do anything to have her own way."

"And you, my friend," broke in Merlin, "don't appear to know your wife as well as you think you do. Magdalyn is a kind, but resourceful woman, and I don't think you give her enough credit."

"Well I, sir, would rather be safe, than sorry. I want my wife back, and I will thank you to unlock this painting so that I can retrieve her . . . by myself, if necessary."

"It will not be necessary to do this on your own. We will all be there to help, but anger will not save Magdalyn. You must retain a cool head, to outwit Maggie, if . . . and I do say if, that is indeed what we must do. Perhaps you underestimate Maggie. Perhaps she is not entirely what you have chosen to believe she is."

Alfred bristled. "You talk treason, Merlin. Maggie is, and has always been, evil, and I cannot see that changing just because you say so."

Merlin sighed. "Alfred, my friend. There's no need to— Let's not jump to conclusions. Perhaps things are not as you now see them, and perhaps they are, but we cannot know that until we can see for ourselves the outcome of this dilemma. Must I leave you here, in the great room, while the rest of us go on to rescue your wife? If you cannot calm down, you may well lead to the destruction of us all. I cannot allow that. It's your choice. Behave yourself or stay here."

Alfred's features softened, but inside he still roiled. Calmly, very calmly he said, "I will do what I can to oblige. I will remain calm as long as I can, but if I find she has done any harm, I cannot, and will not be responsible for my actions."

"Well, noted." Merlin glanced about the room. "Well, are we ready to commence a rescue?"

"Past," Sure-shot grunted. "Let's go, already."

"Ah, yes, young knight. I am charging you with the task of watching out for your grandfather – see that he does not do anything rash. And Brian, son." He whispered, "I am charging you, and Belinda, here, with the task of watching out for the young knight, so that he does not aid his grandfather in his feeble attempt to cause undue problems in this rescue. Understand?"

Resisting the urge to look in his best friend's direction, he nodded slightly, and smiled.

"Good," Merlin said. "We all know where we stand and what we must do . . . or not do, as the case may be. Let us be on our way." With a wave of his hand, and a few well-spoken words, the painting opened, and the small army marched through.

CHAPTER TWENTY-NINE

"Shouldn't they be here by now?" Sarah leaned against an evergreen, and sighed.

"It does seem like it is taking a bit long, but you have to remember, Hatchet is a bit more cumbersome than we are, when it comes to flying. But they'll get here in due time. Let's go back to the meadow. They might already be there." Magdalyn grabbed a stout stick, and began the short trek back to the meadow, with Sarah at her heels. "We must get back to the great room before Alfred does something he shouldn't. I am concerned for Maggie, and Hatchet as well."

"Do you think he would really try to hurt Maggie? And Dad?"

"Without a doubt, if he thought she had done something to hurt me. He is not known for his cool head, or his sweet temper, when he gets angry or scared. We must do what we can to save everyone, including my darling husband, from himself, if necessary, as well as my new sister dragon. And your adopted dad, of course. Hurry, Sarah, time is of the essence." They began to run toward the meadow.

* * *

"She's been here."

"Who?" asked Merlin.

"Magdalyn . . . . and Maggie."

"How can you tell?"

"Her scent is present everywhere, and Magdalyn and I have always had a special connection."

"What about Maggie? Apparently, she can mimic Magdalyn in even subtle ways, or so it seems. She did, after all, confound you when she came back to you pretending to be Magdalyn."

"That is neither here, nor there. I let my emotions cover my good sense. But it won't happen again. I know her tricks, and I will make her pay. Magdalyn is my life, and I will have her back, or Maggie's life will be forfeited, dragon or not."

"Alfred, you are not making sense. I don't think Maggie will actually harm Magdalyn. But I wouldn't put it past her to use her as a hostage. To get to you, I mean."

"If Maggie doesn't bring Magdalyn back in one piece, she is as good as dead. This I promise. She—"

"Dragon! Dragon in the sky."

Alfred searched the sky, half hopeful, half fearful. "Where? I don't see—" But Alfred did see. *Hatchet? Maggie and Hatchet? But where's Magdalyn?* Anger filled his being and his blood began to boil. Forming a ball of magical fire, he threw the missile as hard as he could toward the dragon.

"Alfred, stop!" Merlin screamed, throwing his own fire ball, hoping to deflect the missile nearing the hapless dragon.

Maggie sensed the fireball before she saw it and twisted sideways, the fireball narrowly missing her fragile wing. She heard Hatchet scream as he plummeted toward the ground. In horror, she dove toward the outlaw, scooping him up, and tossing him onto her back, just before they hit the ground. Maggie groaned, her left wing crushed, as Hatchet slid to the ground, and rushed to her head. Cradling the massive head in his arms, he moaned as he rocked back and forth. *No, no, no, not Maggie.*

He caressed her brow as he whispered words of encouragement in her ear. "Don't leave me, Maggie." He cried. "I . . . I love you." Tears poured down his cheeks.

He . . . loves me? Maggie smiled, as best she could, and struggled to open her eyes. *Am I . . . dying?* Her purple tongue slipped out of her mouth, and softly licked the startled outlaw's cheek. "Please . . . don't cry. I . . . love . . . *you . . .* too . . . Will," she whispered, and knew in her heart it was true. Gone were thoughts of Alfred, for she knew now Alfred had been her friend, but he never truly loved her. For all his faults, Hatchet had proven his love time and again. She had just been too blind to see the truth. *Hatchet, Will . . . is a good man . . . but now . . . it is. . . too late. What have . . . I done?*

"Hatchet! Get away from that she-devil."

Hatchet looked up and saw Alfred barreling down upon them, his fingers twitching, a fireball already forming. He gathered Maggie closer and with eyes narrowed said, "My— name—is—Will. Leave her alone . . . Master!"

"Master!? You called me Master after all this time? I knew you would, but it's too late. Now, get away from that monster. She and I have an issue to resolve."

"No! I will not let you harm her!"

"You? *You* will not let *me* harm *her*? She has harmed me more than you know. Move out of the way, or you will die with her. Cousin, or not."

Hatchet glared at the wizard. "I would rather die than let you harm a scale on her beautiful head."

"Then die you will." Alfred raised his hand to drop the outlaw where he knelt, but Hatchet would not budge. "You're a dead man," he bellowed.

Merlin quickly assessed the situation and grabbed Alfred's arm, but he jerked away and proceeded to gather the fireball.

"No," shrieked a terrified voice, as Sarah flew from the

woods and threw herself in front of her 'dad'. Spreading out her arms as far as she could, she shouted, "No, I will not let you kill dad or Maggie. They are my friends."

"And mine!" Magdalyn joined the two protectors and spread her arms wide as well, shielding the outlaw and the suffering dragon as best she could. "Are you alright, Maggie?"

"I am afraid not, my friend. I am dying. I . . . can . . . feel it. I have not . . . the strength . . . to heal . . . with . . . my dragon body. Too . . . large . . .. Not . . . the strength . . . to change into . . . my human . . . form."

"Hang in there, Maggie. We will do what we can to help. With our strength combined with yours maybe, just maybe, we can change the tide."

"I . . . I don't think . . . it will not . . . be enough. I am . . . dying."

"No, you are not!" A voice bellowed from the skies. Looking up, eyes widened, as the sky was filled with a multitude of dragons, large and small. At the front of the army, Robert sat astride Ellie, observing this standoff between his stymied father, the injured Maggie, and her would be rescuers, including his mother. *Mother?* Something strange was going on, and his parents were right in the middle of it.

Ellie glided swiftly, but silently, toward the ground, and landed in front of the rescue party, wings spread open wide in protection. Robert slid to the ground and stood by Ellie.

"Robert, get out of the way. Come join me and bring your mother with you. Maggie has obviously confounded your mother's mind. She must pay for her sins." At Robert's hesitation, he stomped his foot and again demanded. "As your father, I order you to join me . . . now. And bring your mother, whether she wants to come or not. I will not lose her again."

"Father . . . listen to yourself. You sound like you have lost your mind. Calm yourself and be reasonable. Merlin?"

"I have tried, Robert, but he refuses to listen. I will do my best to attend to your father, but right now I think Maggie needs you more."

"Traitor!" Alfred glared, but knowing he was no match for the senior wizard, allowed himself to be led away to a nearby log, and grudgingly took a seat.

"Robert, quickly. We must all work together to save her."

Robert turned and joined hands with the others, lightly touching Maggie, as Ellie shifted and covered them all with her wings. "Do what you must, Maggie," Ellie whispered.

Gathering strength from those surrounding her, Maggie

concentrated on becoming human. Moments later, a beautiful black woman with purple streaks in her hair, lay quivering in Hatchet's arms.

"If I may be so bold." Merlin joined this odd group and laid a hand on Maggie's forehead. Her body began to relax, and she grew still.

Alfred rose and cautiously walked toward this strange scene. "Maggie?" he asked. He took his wife's hand in his. "Magdalyn? What is going on here? Is this woman indeed Maggie? My Maggie?"

"Yes, Alfred. This is Maggie, your one-time dragon, and my friend. I love you, Alfred, but I can't let you destroy her. She has become family."

"I—I didn't know. I'm sorry . . . so sorry. But . . . it looks like she has become Hatchet's family as well."

"My—name—is—Will," the outlaw reminded, his eyes on the beauteous Maggie.

"Hmmm. Well, cousin, it seems things have changed. I don't understand, but—" He laid his hand on his cousin's shoulder and the outlaw was filled with warmth and strength. His mangled foot tingled and he stared at the rapidly straightening foot and leg. "Master?"

"There's no need to call me master, anymore. You are your own man, and have been for some time, it seems.

Besides, if the women in my life find you worthy, who am I to earn their wrath, by condemning you." He grinned. "I release you to find your own happiness." He turned toward Magdalyn. "Is that alright with you, my love."

"Perfectly, my darling husband. You really are the wonderful man I married." She smiled and drew him into her arms.

EPILOGUE

The great room was alive once again. Tables and couches were pushed against the walls, and row after row of comfortable chairs graced the center of the room. Huge sprays of flowers adorned the far end of the room, just in front of the castle painting, and Todd was excitedly issuing orders as to what the right and proper placing should be. At each end, of every row, large satin bows surrounded a lovely bouquet of roses and daisies.

The Fairy Queen directed her subjects as they lit the upper candles, and then settled on the various bouquets. All their friends and family were present, as well as representatives from all the painted realms. Belinda smiled and waved a tiny wave to Kelp and Pearl as she took her place, near the alter, as bridesmaid. Sarah, as junior bridesmaid, stood next to Belinda and held tightly to Amanda Joy's hand as the tiny flower girl continued to toss flower petals everywhere. Sure-shot grinned at Belinda as he stood opposite her as an usher. Professor Hawthorn stood proudly next to Sure-shot. It was a great day. Then . . ..

The musicians began to play. It was time.

* * *

Brian stood proudly as best man, and Bee happily took *her* place as matron of honor. Her best friend was getting married, and it was about time.

Being a widow for so long, Gwenny never thought it possible she would find love again. But here he stood, by her side, handsome, debonair, and he loved her.

Merlin couldn't believe his good fortune. Not only was he getting a beautiful woman for his wife, but also a fabulous cook. He had never felt this way about anyone, not even the lady of the lake. He was in love, and about to be married to the woman of his dreams. And, he was getting a mighty fine grandson in the bargain. He glanced toward Brian and received a grin in return. He was happy, the family was happy, and even Alfred and Magdalyn were happy.

He glanced toward the castle painting, where Maggie and Will stood, watching, smiling and watching. They had been invited to the wedding, of course, but Maggie was too ashamed, for what she had tried to do, and didn't really want to intrude. So, they stood on the outskirts, happy to be a part, if but from a distance, of this blessed affair. Magdalyn smiled at Maggie, and gestured for her to come in, but she was content to watch from where she stood.

Merlin gripped Gwenny's hand and stood a little straighter as the ceremony began. This was it, and he was content.

* * *

Maggie gazed up at Hatchet, and softly repeated the words spoken by Gwenny, "I, Maggie, take you, Will . . ." and Will did the same . . . when the time was right. "I really do love you," she whispered, "Will . . .."

And Will smiled back, happy to be with the woman/dragon he loved.

* * *

For the first time in many years, Gwenny was not in charge of the festive meal. She longed to add her two-cents worth into the pot but knew that she could never offend Bee, Magdalyn, and Amanda Hawthorn, her newest old friend. They seemed so happy to be able to do this for her, she just couldn't take it away from them. But then again, when would she have had the time?

She looked up as her new husband rose to make a toast to the light of his life. Who would have ever thought that she would marry a wizard? The kindest, most adorable wizard in the world, and he loved her. . . as much as she loved him.

She smiled at Bee and then brought her attention back to

her new husband. Merlin . . . her husband. Who would have ever thought? The light of true love shone in her eyes and she was happy.

Previous books in "The Gift" series

Book one

The Gift

Book two

Merlin's   Revenge

Book Three

The Revealing

Book four

In the Beginning
Todd

Book Five

The Final Battle

Chapter Book

Treasure at
Mermaid's Cove

Prequel

Book one

The Girl with the
Sky-Blue Eyes

Book two

Return from
Dragon Island